The Street of Mists

The Street of Mists

Mariam Karim

Vitasta
Let Knowledge Spread

Times Group Books

Published by
Renu Kaul Verma for
Vitasta Publishing Pvt. Ltd.
2/15, Ansari Road, Daryaganj,
New Delhi - 110 002
info@vitastapublishing.com

ISBN 978-81-925354-1-8

Layout and Cover Design by Vitasta Publishing Pvt. Ltd.
Printed by Vits Press, New Delhi

Marketed and Distributed exclusively in India & Sub-Continent by:

Times Group Books

Times Group Books
(A division of Bennett, Coleman and Company Limited)
Times Annexe, Express Building
9-10 Bahadur Shah Zafar Marg, New Delhi-110 002

To

all those who seek alternate
realities, and survive.

ACKNOWLEDGEMENTS

I wish to thank the Cultural Service of the French Embassy in New Delhi and the Egide in Paris, for all the help rendered in connection with the Residency in 2005 during which I collected material and insights for this novel.

Special thanks to Myriam Rasiwala for her support.

CONTENTS

Prologue

The Creator made the world, they say, and the Created made Art. Therefore, when we speak of Life and Art, Life precedes Art, and Art is subordinate to Life. But then the definition of Art is established by the Created… what if we deemed Art to precede Life? Considered Art the "Primary Phenomenon"? Its significance would change, would it not?

Art has a life of its own, experienced or not by a sentient examiner. It is an interactive reality. Even visual art, which has to sit literally at the feet of Reality, is a mere reflection. The creation of fine music continues to have a mysticism attached to it, and little is said of environmental or genetic factors which may be responsible… for such beauty, such transport, a gift in this ugly world, must only be felt, perceived, not analyzed.

Visual art, however, has sociological parameters, within which it is considered to exist, and that connoisseurs are supposed to know at a glance: the elements are recognizable, referable to some external reality, if nothing, at least to form, or to non-form, or colour.

The life of a painting has been seriously underrated… yes, it contains philosophy, politics, emotion, aesthetics, and those strange interactive elements we sometimes refer to as inspiration, but the source of these is unknown—for little electrical impulses running over the earth can act upon an artist's person… and bits of knowledge, bits of perhaps unimportant information get translated upon a canvas…

I
CONJUGATING THE VERB

Today there's a lot of *va-et-vient* on the street my window looks out onto. The theatre's first show. *L'Atalante*. And the Japanese woman's arm is taken by the balding Frenchman, while the tall grey-haired one carries his wife's purse as though it were a nest of hornets. Long coats are fashionable and I have a black one I shall wear when I meet Fabrice tomorrow at Berthillon's at the Ile St-Louis. It's too cold for sorbets this summer, though.

Each of us is assigned a life, I believe. Why my life couldn't have been someone else's, is because I was assigned this life and I have to live it out. So I turned twenty-one last October, and when I got on the plane I was asking myself, whose life am I following, my grandmother's, my mother's, or my own? Who am I, of these three women? But the moment my father's face appears before me, I know it is my own life. Because however closely you may identify with your parents, you know that your joys and sorrows, gains and losses have to be your own.

I lost very early two of the most important people in my life, two powerful loves, my mother, and Rahul. He was one for whom my heart will yearn forever… my mother, I had to finally learn to live without, as does everyone, but I yet had to learn to live with Rahul, when he was taken from me. An accident that happened to my life. Mine alone.

Paris is a timeless city. Or is it a city caught in time? Like a flower in a candle made of glycerine and clear wax, immovable, glowing … and the people, repeating their days, over, over, over again, walking the same boulevards, frequenting the same cafés, haunting the same hotels, traversing the same gardens, exactly the same as my mother had described to me. Is this what she longed for? For these unchanging tableaux, so anguished her soul? Walked away into nothingness? No, surely not. These people, who seem like moving pictures to me, must have had human faces for her.

The *remue-ménage* gets louder under my window. The old proprietor of the vegetarian restaurant with his absurd chef's cap is trying to woo an older lady with silver hair and a long checked coat. Perhaps she will live another few years if she eats vegetables.

I like Montmartre better than the Left Bank, after all. Or perhaps I have just learnt to appreciate the present, that which *is*. My mother was held captive by her past. Will I be able to free her?

Then there's Fabrice. My skin doesn't ache to touch his, as it did Rahul's.

Rahul. Will my past hold me captive too, forever? Or is it too early to tell? When Fabrice holds my hand, it just doesn't feel right.

Now the crowd has gone into the theatre. Women on immaculate heels, in fine shoes, sheer stockings, but with lined faces, like masks, elegant ones, as though on young people, with tousled hair.

Tomorrow will not be sunny. Up the hill of Montmartre the air is fresher. Now I can hear the dialogues floating up from the theatre. I've lived with theatre since I can remember: our house back in India is called *Isfahan*, after the exotic Iranian city, and if that isn't theatrical enough, bent old Qamrun *Bua* does her rounds, imprecating, unmindful of time and occasion!

Four loud boys with cigarettes behind their ears are being aggressive with each other. Like our *rickshawallahs* with their *bidis* behind their ears.

A "good boy" passes by, in his tie and glasses and ignores the louts who are standing against the wall. Soon someone will appear from the theatre and ask them to leave.

***

The morning is pleasant, after all. Windy, I think, as the plant on the balcony of the building across is swaying pretty fiercely. Must be a woman who lives up there; there's a looking glass that reflects the early morning sun. And from the glass, Sylvia Plath's 'terrible fish' must be rising up to meet her. The calls of the blackbirds in the trees of the square are mesmerizing, as they echo round the corridors of sound and air created between the closely set buildings.

There are sparrows too, cheeping. At the Notre Dame garden, there'd been this odd middle-aged American woman who was having her picture taken with a few dirty sparrows eating out of her hand. And everyone was making much of her; she looked so obviously American, with a smile too wide, large baubles in her ears, and hair dyed blonde. "Doing Paris." It was the energy and the money, I suppose, that she had to spend. And I thought of Roxana, the new maid back home at *Isfahan*, trying to chase away the pesky sparrows as she cleaned the wheat. She has five children and her second husband has refused to support her.

Fabrice says, though, that Paris has changed over the past twenty years alone. Men have become uglier, for one; women have given up putting on make-up and started having babies. They've even started talking to their babies in public, which only the Arabs did earlier. Fabrice can be funny!

I told Fabrice that I have come to Paris to solve the enigma of my mother's life. If I can. For my own sake. I want to breathe the air she breathed, see the places she saw, live as she lived, so perhaps her death might begin to make sense to me, and I may become closer to her. Her death—an unnecessary sacrifice. I understand now that it *was* my father's fear that led to everything. My dear, lovely Daddy! He lived, grew up in a town that trembled, day after day, with the fear of 'the other'. A town politically alive with fear–the fear of those who wish to annihilate you. The Hindus feared the Muslims and the Muslims feared the Hindus. My father is fighting a difficult battle, although he wants to deny the existence of a battle, on the face of it. My mother found it easier, to dismiss it all as absurd, which it is, actually. Fear is the real enemy; it makes Reality Absurd, and it can kill you, as it did Rahul.

***

In the metro, a harassed couple sat with their three children. The youngest, a girl, howled incessantly. She was parked on her father's lap. The eldest, a girl again, sat looking out of the window into the darkness, as though she found it very interesting. She was about ten. The middle child, a boy, was seated across his father with his little sister's feet kicking at his knees as she howled.

The father was bullying the youngster: "What is *je suis*?" (I am)

The young man put his forefinger into his mouth and mumbled something inaudible. The father's voice became menacing. "WHAT IS *JE SUIS*?"

The boy took his finger out of his mouth and said haltingly, "*Je suis venu.*" I have come.

"*Non! Non! Non!*" cried the incensed father. "That is the *passé compose* of the verb *venir*, 'to come'. *Je suis* is the verb *être*, 'to be', in the present tense!"

The little sister, as if on cue, suddenly caterwauled and kicked frantically, straining towards the mother, who sat diagonally opposite.

"*Non, non,*" said the mother. "I cannot. I am busy." She purposefully nursed the steel flask on her lap. "*Je suis occupée.*" *Je suis*. I am. To be. The importance of conjugating the verb correctly. The sheer absurdity of the preoccupation with the conjugated verb. The child didn't understand, just as her brother didn't.

To tell the truth, I want to tell my life back at *Isfahan*, "*Je suis occupée.*" I am busy. I want time to be myself. I thought I would go to London, to look for Qadeer Mamoon, my grandmother's best friend. But my sense of purpose was dealt a severe blow by the fact that Qadeer Mamoon, who could have told me all about my grandmother and my mother's life as a child, was away in Pakistan, visiting a dying cousin. He would be away for many weeks, and it wasn't certain when he would return. He was old, and unwell, with some gradually worsening disease, and he was away. I could neither do anything for him, nor learn anything from him.

And then, Paris is such a beautiful city, like a jewel set so carefully. I felt like a ship that wants to cast anchor. To drift for a while, as the past, the present, the future all mingle. I could just *be.* And say, *je suis. I am.*

***

As for Fabrice, how long shall I last with him? I can't sleep with him, no not yet at least, and he, I think, will tire of me soon, because for him a relationship without sex is ... well...leading nowhere. At twenty-one, a virgin, he cries! *C'est extra*! But he doesn't think this state should continue, however grand it may be!

"And there are, nevertheless, emancipated Indian women too!" he said one day.

"I think we differ on the meaning of emancipation, Fabrice,"

I told him, trying to be polite. He was a friend, I needed him. He would help me in my quest.

"Why, look at that Indian *actrice* that just came to Cannes, she lived with a *mec français.*"

"Is it the only form of emancipation for an Indian woman—to live with a Frenchman?" I was trying hard not to lose my cool.

"Well, darling, with your ideas of arranged marriages and your bourgeois life…"

"You put that thing about arranged marriages in yourself."

"That's what good Indian girls are supposed to do, right?"

"Fabrice, look, is emancipation supposed to mean empowerment, or not?"

"You have the power to choose whether you want to *baiser* with a Frenchman," he shrugged meaningfully.

"That's a vulgar word, Fabrice, for making love, and you know it."

"Oh, *là là*! Always the little Miss *Bourgeoise*! You know, I did see that Bollywood film, *Bride and Prejudice*, and do have an idea of what Indian girls want."

Now it was my turn to say 'Oh *là, là*!', "You are supposed to be intelligent, Fabrice. Do I really seem like one of the girls in the film?"

"*Non*," he looked defeated, for some reason, and we ordered another sorbet. It had been a silly, juvenile conversation. The wind blew through our sweaters, and we shivered. A young couple hugged and kissed just in front of us, and I thought in this cold it would not be so bad to be hugged by Fabrice after all. He was quite good looking, in a very French way, and his face was sensitive, again in a very French way, and his hands were long and clean cut. He had very green eyes, often flecked with brown and his hair had a tendency towards red, although he was not freckled.

"Look Fabrice," I said, "In India, there are many poor and very backward people, who, according to you, would be emancipated.

There are tribal and other groups who have very open sexual mores. They may also smoke, and drink alcohol, without being considered wicked or loose."

"*Voilà*," said Fabrice, smiling engagingly, "*Les femmes émancipées*!"

"But ask them, Fabrice, would they swear never to have sex again, never to touch another *bidi*, never to drink again, if they were offered a house, a car, a job where they were respected, enough money to support, educate and feed their children, a husband, perhaps who gave them a place in society? They would swear, in a minute, and never look back."

Fabrice looked crestfallen. "They would swear never to have *sex*?"

I couldn't help smiling. He was rather endearing, looking as he did.

"Respect in society is more important. The power to never be in a position to beg anything of anyone; the power to not be open to aggression, within or without the family."

"You are studying sociology, no doubt." The corners of his mobile mouth turned down, and he nodded his head in mock seriousness.

"Don't make fun of me, Fabrice," I said, tongue-in-cheek, "or you'll never be able to seduce me."

The wind blew in grey clouds, and we decide to walk a little. On the small bridge between the Ile Saint-Louis and the Notre Dame Cathedral, a violinist played a gay melody. The smell of crêpes wafted up from nowhere. And of ground coffee. A small crowd collected around the violinist, a slim girl with her hair tied up in a matter-of-fact way and torn shoes. She seemed lost in the music. The cathedral bells sounded, and mingled with the music. The magic of Paris was surrounding me from all sides, like a thin vapour, entering my pores, like a flavour, like a drug, like a sticky string of gossamer, impossible to detach.

***

The discussion on emancipation hung between us at every meeting. For Fabrice, emancipation meant being able to do what pleases you, with your body, without any morality attached. That is what I gathered.

Then one afternoon I met some really emancipated men, "*types très émancipés,*" I told Fabrice later. I was at the *butte* Montmartre,and all my anger was directed at Fabrice, who pretended to have the answer to everything, for a reason I could not immediately identify. It had something to do with racism, and with sex, and degradation, but I couldn't put a finger on it.

I had decided to take a walk up to where the carrousel is, at the end of Rue d'Orsel, and then a little further up towards the Basilica of the Sacré-Coeur, which stands out whitely, pointing upwards, an unusual cumulo-nimbus about to lose its balance and fall forward down the hill.

I sat down on one of the benches, looking down at the carrousel. The music floated up, and I set my face against the wind, happy to just *be*, and wonder where my life was taking me. An Asian woman came and sat down next to me. She couldn't have been forty … I thought of my mother. A group of young black men hung around the steps.Suddenly one of them approached me and asked me to stick out my index finger… he looked harmless enough and I held out my finger. The man started to wind some coloured strings around it, saying something like "*Bayou-bayou-haramba*!" A manner of greeting people in Africa, he said.

"He will ask for money now," said the lady next to me.

He wound the strings into a pretty friendship band then caressed my finger with one of his, saying "Massage", which was soon over, following which he put it around my wrist.

"Now he'll ask for money," said the lady.

"Only for a *café crème*," said the man.

The lady took the band off my wrist, put it around the black man's wrist, and said, "Now *you* give *me* for a *café crème*!"

The man quickly went away, but soon after the lady departed he was back by my side.

"What's your name?" I asked.

"George Washington," he said.

"No," I said, "not possible."

"Everyone calls themselves George Washington in Sierra Leone," he said, "because he was a very educated man."

"Yes," I replied, "education is important."

"My real name is Jhalloh, I am a student," he said. "Do you have a *petit ami*..." he said, edging closer to me on the bench, "... a boyfriend?"

"No," I said, for want of something to say quickly, "I am married, my family wouldn't approve."

"Oh," he said, "but this is France. Everyone can do everything. Where do you come from? Delhi?"

"Around," I answered.

"There are many religions in India, what are you? Buddhist? Hindu?"

"I'm a Muslim," I said. "*Je suis Musulmane.*"

He looked taken aback. "*Musulmane*?" I had in some way discomfited him. His cavalier manner evaporated, and he looked pensive.

"Bizarre," he said, "I too am a Muslim."

I was going to win this one I thought–I put the adjective triumphantly after the conjugated verb *je suis*, "I am a Muslim. *Je suis Musulmane.*"

He wouldn't have guessed it, he said.

"Being a Muslim doesn't mean having a scarf around your head," I said. "Islam is a religion of *Ikhlaq*. You say you can do anything in Paris, does the Quran say you can do anything?" .... he looked suitably defeated, I thought.

He seemed to be listening quite seriously and I felt elated. I had taken him to be a lost soul.

Abruptly he cried, "Excuse me!"

I looked in the direction of his flight ... all the young men had collected in a group after having bullied a group of Swedish students into the *Bayou-bayou-haramba* game, and the one in the middle had an erect penis sticking out of his pants, while another tied a coloured friendship band around it.

I turned my face and descended the stairs swiftly. I could hear some angry voices and some laughter floating down behind me. I lost myself in the crowd on the Rue d'Orsel, hoping George Washington wasn't following.

"See!" I cried later to Fabrice, "What colonization has done to men. They have no self-respect, no culture to call their own; they don't know what their religion is! See what you whites have done to the black people!"

"Don't take it so hard, *chérie*," Fabrice said equably. "You're not responsible for everything that's wrong in the world."

"But don't you feel responsible, in the least responsible, for everything your 'emancipated' race has done? When you have to take the credit for Thomas Edison's inventions or for the Wright brothers having invented the airplane, you don't say your famous '*Bof* ... you feel very proud, then why don't you accept your disgrace as well?"

"Darling, of course it is a shame; it's all the fallout of our colonial past, but will fighting with *me* help in any way?" He shrugged his shoulders in a very French way. I knew he was right. I felt very young compared to him at that moment. He was several years older than I, maybe eight, Rahul's age.

"All I want to do is to make love with you ..." his voice was velvety. "I am not racist, see? I love Indian women."

"Stop it, Fabrice!"

He sighed. "Oh, you young people!"

"All I am asking is an honest opinion," I said.

"Well, I'll tell you once, then don't ask me again. The thing is, I think, that like different races of ants, for example, we have different tendencies. There is a species of ants that attacks other anthills, and takes the soldier ants of the besieged hill prisoner then takes them back to their own hill and makes them do their work. Can you accept that human beings may be like that? That different races of human beings may actually have tendencies to behave differently? And that history and sociology and anthropology may just be mistaken, when they say all human races are the same in essence? Although we all came out of Africa, they say … I am not making an excuse for inhuman behaviour, please understand. It's just my way of trying to make sense of it."

"I'm sorry," I said quickly.

"On a large scale the white races have destroyed other civilizations but on an individual level they try and make up for it. They go deep into uninhabitable areas of countries their compatriots have destroyed and run schools, hospitals. Can they assuage the colonial guilt? Who knows? But they are treated so well in these places that the spiritual rewards they get are far greater than the physical hardships they suffer. At least it shows that the individual is not always a part of a larger system. He can be different if he wants …"

He suddenly grabbed my hand. "You have some of the colonizers blood too. You can colonize me anytime you like!" I let him hold my hand.

"As for being young, Fabrice, I'm ancient, in a way, from all the sorrow I have massed inside me. When it lets me go, I shall be myself again."

He still held my hand. He said nothing, but I felt a warmth emanating from him that reassured me.

"You told me about your mother," he said after a bit, "But not what happened to your boyfriend."

"Rahul was eight years older than me. A journalist. He had been commissioned to investigate a case of the molestation of a catholic nun by extremists. He was on the right track. They murdered him. With a block of the stone being used to construct a place of worship."

2
Dodi, the Beloved

From the hotel, I shifted into a building, a vertiginous one, triangular in shape, a little up the hill. All the buildings there seem to be converging at some point; of course it is just an impression given by the fact that they are on a hill and built in the typical Parisian way. One close by, on the Rue des Norvins, No 22, now known as the Folie Sandrin, used to be a home for the mentally ill, where a doctor thought that kindness was the best cure, at a time when new drugs were being used to experiment on the depressed and the mentally unbalanced. That was Doctor Prost, disciple of Pinel, who said that the treatment of the morale of patients was the key to their healing. Kindliness and benevolence would first win the confidence of the patients, and then lead them to a definitive cure.

The well-known writer Gérard de Nerval had recuperated from a nervous illness at this same place. Recuperated for a while. Gérard de Nerval, who searched for the eternal feminine, for a lost mother, and who knew madness had him in its grip, who lived in a dream-world, more real to him than reality.

Yet, in the old French tale, Alphonse Daudet's *La Chevre de*

Monsieur Séguin, (Monsieur Séguin's Goat), the goats wanted to be free, and the old goatherd thought he could keep them from running away to the mountains and being eaten by the wolf if he loved them enough. Freedom and love are both important to human beings too, and one cannot replace the other. In fact, like the goats, one often chooses freedom over love. At whatever cost.

Before Pinel discarded the belief, mental illness was considered to be the result of demoniacal possession. Doctor Pinel, in 1801, freed mentally ill patients in Paris from chains and shackles. He started visiting the privately confined, emotionally and spiritually disturbed after a friend of his ran away into the countryside in 1785 and was eaten by wolves. Like the goats of Monsieur Séguin, his friend had found liberation, perhaps.

I press the numbers for the door to open. A2345. Like Alibaba's cave, the door stands ajar even before I can finish. A young man with a balding head and a vacant expression is standing in the doorway, taking out his bicycle. He looks at me with pale blue eyes, directly.

"I have been waiting for you," he said. There was nothing sinister about his statement, as his face was guileless, and I asked, "Really? Why?"

He continued edging his bicycle out of the doorway, "I will come back and tell you," he said. I shrugged and went upstairs to my suite of rooms, very small, very Parisian. The French windows looked out onto a clump of trees where birds could be heard. Roses were in heavy bloom all over the boundary wall, and sent wafts of fragrance into my bedroom in the early morning. It had been very kind of Monsieur Houllebecq to let me stay in his apartment while he was away. Monsieur Houllebecq is a sort of an artist, a painter, in his fifties, who is known to my grandmother's publisher. He lives alone, and in the early summer takes off to a little village in the hills above Monaco to paint. And to regain his health, he says. I met him only briefly, when he gave me the keys and kissed my hand. A free apartment in Paris–I had been very lucky.

The next time I encountered the pale young man in the doorway he did not wish me, let alone say he had been waiting for me; I thought he had obviously mistaken me for someone else the first time.

***

The light in Paris is quite extraordinary. The colour, the texture it lends to the yellow and grey stone buildings, the way it reflects off them; surely all this has an effect on the mind that urges it towards creativity. But there is something sad, and sombre, and knowing, in the eyes of the people, something perhaps which they gather within them in the winter, the traces of which remain despite the gaiety when the warm summer days arrive.

I bought myself a box of water colours and a few sheets of paper to go with them. I had a canvas, a good one, and a set of expensive oils, but I didn't want to use them until I had something serious to paint. An easel is too dear. So I begged one off an Italian cartoonist, Bernardo, and his wife Anita, who spend the summer doing portraits at the Place du Tertre, which is within walking distance from where I now live. I just got talking to them, and Italians seem quite like Indians, and they make friends easily. Before the tourists arrive, they allow me the use of their easels. I also ask them for tips on painting, and Bernardo is quite a learned man, he knows the tales, and the techniques, of all the Italian and French painters. Sometimes I paint in my room but the views don't change there, and after a point I need to go out and walk about. I still cannot paint from memory. To tell the truth, when I see all these artists at the Place du Tertre, I seriously begin to doubt my own talent. But if practice does help, I'm going to practice for all I'm worth!

Back home in India, in the sleepy little town of Rahimganj, a town with big dreams that never materialized, Daddy gets worried if I don't phone once a day. I asked him to come over, but he said he has a lot of work at the newspaper. He hasn't been himself actually, since Mummy left us and I wonder what I can do to help him. I'll go back to India soon. I don't know if I can ever find the people my mother was looking for. Maybe I can come again later. Daddy will worry a lot if I stay longer. He knows Fabrice's father, who is a friend of my grandmother's publisher, has promised to take care of me. But if he knew how Fabrice has started to feel about me, he would throw a purple fit.

***

Although the strange young man in the doorway didn't speak to me after that, I had a weird feeling up my spine about him. I saw him once or twice with his bicycle, coming and going with fresh bread from the *boulangerie*, or some other shopping; he looked through me, and I felt myself shiver. You're just imagining things, I said to myself. It's being alone, for the first time in your life. Really alone, in an apartment, to shop, cook, and roam around as you please… an (almost) emancipated woman. But, certainly there is something about this boy that's a bit extraordinary, I countered to myself. I'm not really one for imagining things.

It was late one night, when I was returning from a lively discussion with Bernardo and Anita at the Place du Tertre, I heard some loud voices as I entered the inner courtyard. A door opened on the ground floor, and the odd young man rushed out, cursing in French. Behind him came a slightly portly but extremely well attired woman, with a fine face and very black eyes. She had her hair done up in a chignon, and she wore pearls around her neck.

"*Mais, non*, Dodi!" she cried, in French, "You don't have to leave! Think about it, go in the morning!"

Dodi saw me and stopped in his tracks. "It's her again!" he said, as though seeing me after a long time, although we had often crossed each other since our first meeting.

"*Pardon*?" I said

"I knew you would have something to do with it all!" cried Dodi angrily. "All this is happening because you had to come." The freckles on his face stood out, even in the semi darkness.

"Dodi, leave the girl alone, what has she to do with anything!" said the lady.

"*Maman*, you know I know many things you don't," said Dodi patiently.

The mother turned to me, with a worried expression. "Please excuse us, I am sorry."

"No, it's perfectly alright," I said.

"Come and have tea with me once we sort this out. I live here; my door's on the ground floor."

"Thank you," I said

Dodi seemed to relent, and shuffled quickly back into the house, even before his mother could step back. The heavy door shut to, and I went up to my apartment, baffled.

***

My strange meeting with Dodi was the beginning of a relationship that neither I nor his mother could have foreseen. Not between Dodi and me, no, of course not, but between me and the whole family. Although his mother did not want to give credence to Dodi's utterances, she did not whole-heartedly reject them either.

A few days later I was invited to tea.

As soon as I entered, I was introduced to a small person called Monsieur Manès Trigot. I say "small person" not because he was young, no, he must have been in his thirties, but because he was short and slim, with a square head, and a plaintive expression in his wide-set, pale blue eyes, as well as about his mouth. His arms were short and muscular, his hands square and small, always held at some angle to the wrist, (a position that heightened the impression of lament), and changed to and fro in harmony with the tilt of his head. His hair was brown, with a tendency to curl, and looked untidy the moment he tilted his head. A hundred images of untidiness, I said to myself. But Madame Desmoulins, Dodi's mother, said he was very kind, *gentil*, because he offered to help repair the roof when it leaked, and helped Dodi with his math on Wednesday evenings. Monsieur Trigot got up to shake my hand, but he was not much taller standing than sitting. As he rose, I noticed behind him a framed photograph of Salvador Dali's winged snail with an angel on its back.

Dodi shuffled in from the kitchen, in slippers, with his oddly curtailed movements of arms and head, like the marionette of an amateur puppeteer. He sat down next to Monsieur Manès on the sofa and pointed me out with an indecisive gesture of his hand. "It's her," he said. Monsieur Manès nodded, head tilted sideways, sadly. "Sure it is," he replied. I looked around for Madame Desmoulins, who represented the only element of sanity in the room. She was there, putting out the tea things and *petits-fours*, and *viennoiserie* in the form of raisin bread and croissants, on the small square table covered with a soiled white tablecloth. Once again I admired the aquiline nose, the gentle curve of her mouth and the childlike innocence of her dark eyes.

The tea was served in expensive but chipped enamel; it was actually tea, not coffee. I had always been invited for "*un petit café*", so tea was a novelty. Only the initiated served tea.

"Excuse me for receiving you in the *petit salon*," she said, "The bigger one has not been dusted."

Monsieur Manès looked sadly at the croissant to which he

had helped himself, then broke off a piece and put it in his mouth. Dodi addressed himself to me in second person for the first time, "The snail is me, and the angel is Monsieur Manès Trigot," he said pointing to the Dali photograph.

"Oh," I said, sagely nodding my head, not daring to look in the least inquiring, "Of course."

There was a small silence, as we sat around the table, the four of us. "Oh, yes," chirped Madame Desmoulins, "Dodi loves Dali. He goes to the private museum at the Espace Montmartre, by the Place du Tertre, so often that they let him in without a ticket now."

Dodi nodded seriously. "Yes, I know the works by heart: *Abraham, Crucifixion, Alice, the Melted Clock, the Unicorn, the Universe of Pantagruel, the Dancers...*"

"*Oui, oui,*" Monsieur Manès interrupted him with surprising authority. "Now if you have finished your tea, go get your math book."

The voice of a child came from upstairs, and that of a mother answering in subdued tones. Dodi looked disconcerted, even angry. A light colour mounted his cheeks.

"That's 'The Shadow,' he said darkly, to me, '*L'Ombre*'. He got up to leave and the other two threw no light on his statement by their silence.

The child called again, more demanding this time. Madame Desmoulins' eyes went to the stairway. Dodi had left.

"Don't mind Dodi," she said apologetically, "He's not all there, you know. Not all there at all." She sounded sad, which was natural, I thought. Monsieur Trigot contemplated a crack on his teacup, eyebrows knit, as though it was all the fault of the teacup.

I went home and drew a caricature of Monsieur Manès Trigot in overalls, falling off the roof, with a cracked teacup in his hand. It was brilliant. It pleased me so much I found it difficult to fall asleep!

***

The world Fabrice inhabited, on the other hand, was very different from that of the people I came to know at Montmartre. There were *soirées* to which I was invited, that tinkled with the sound of champagne and other wines being poured into gleaming glasses accompanied by the well-bred laughter of well-dressed women. There were well-travelled men and women who had an opinion on everything. They had many words to express those opinions, many glowing experiences of other countries including India, which made them genuinely believe they were the chosen of the earth, which perhaps they were. The joys and sorrows of the world seemed to touch them only at the level of the intellect, or not at all. To be emotional about anything was ill-bred, save spiritual experience induced by travel, save the beauty or the ugliness of other nations, their aesthetic value, so to speak. As if other nations and other people existed by virtue of the role they played in the lives of these people. Politics too, was a favourite subject, the plight of the industrial workers, Sarkozy, and a common Constitution for Europe. Did any one of them know or care that Dodi existed?

Fabrice introduced me to all his friends. He held my arm possessively. It seemed to me that he didn't want to lose me to someone else before I had accepted his advances!

"You're always shy and quiet," he said, at one party, taking me to a corner. The intimacy of his touch on my arm, the nearness of his face, overwhelmed me a bit. The odour of his perfume mixed with that of Muscadet, the concern in his green eyes–a Frenchman living up to his reputation of being seductive.

"My French isn't good," I said, by way of an excuse, "I am always conscious of the mistakes I make."

"Nobody is going to penalize you for your bad French," he said, "and unless you speak you will never get over your shyness."

"I tend to think people consider you are stupid if you can't find the right words in their language. Especially the French. It's like you're retarded or something. They start explaining things to you that you understand perfectly, except that you haven't been able to express it in the perfect sentence. "

He laughed loudly, and rested his head on my shoulder, "*Petite bête!*" he said, "Stupid girl!" He sighed and looked up. "Why don't you want me the way I want you?"

"It's just that I'm not brought up with the idea of wanting a man like this," I said, partly dishonestly, because the feeling I had experienced for Rahul certainly consisted of a deep craving, physical as well as emotional.

· Not in the least put out, he took my arm and led me to the dance floor, where he held me close, saying not a word as we moved to the music. I tried to keep my mind off his fragrance and his proximity, which was difficult as I had had a glass of champagne. "One day you will long for me, too," he whispered, letting me go when the number was over

I could not bring myself to talk to Fabrice about Madame Desmoulins and Dodi and The Shadow. I thought he would consider them lowly, pitiable, not interesting enough. Perhaps I was stupid, ignoring the advances of a rich and handsome Frenchman, and wasting my thoughts on the miseries of a strange boy and his mother. But I couldn't help it. The upper class seemed so complete, so contained. I could only view them from the exterior, there was no chink which would allow me to break into that apparently perfect harmony in their lives; of course I knew that perfect harmony does not exist, but the possibility of harmony, lets say, is greater. While in a life like Dodi's, like Madame Desmoulins', it is an impossibility.

I had gone to see the exhibition of Matisse's découpage works and the letters he had written to André Rouveyre, at the Musée du Luxembourg. I thought I could discuss that with a smart lady with a cigarette. But she had so many words for it in French, that what I had to say didn't seem interesting any longer. I tried to say that the perfection of unlike things put together in complete accord had made a strong impression on me, but she snatched my words as they left my tongue, and made new sentences of them and I was again silent. It wasn't an interesting conversation after all. I excused myself and decided to listen in to the men talking about the Constitution, a Referendum. I did not even try to give an opinion, and happily sipped my drink.

It was true, in his world of ease and comfort, of Saint-Germain-des-Prés, politics could be discussed vociferously, emotion was acceptable at a distance, acceptable in love as in sex, acceptable in appreciation of exotic places, in the perfect pictures of misery of India or Bangladesh, but when something is as close to you as your neighbour, as the mean distress of the homeless on the street outside, the old drunkard lying fallen on the bench in the nearby park, the young jobless junkies smoking a joint around the corner, the madwoman at the Gare du Nord following the pigeons and screaming, all these were too commonplace to discuss or to get emotional about. Never, never, could I start a discussion with the lady with the cigarette and the many words to express her bright ideas. It seemed the two worlds were estranged and alienated irreparably; hermetised from each other by invisible barriers that could and would never be crossed; and I, an alien, could pass easily through them, unseen.I had not the cultural body nor soul to be stopped by them…and I found myself caught in cold draughts. However, the occasional sunshine bright on the trees remained the same, the music in the metros played on, only the music, like me, easily crossed the undefined line between the two worlds, while the scruffy musician remained on one side of the barrier.

***

Each morning I lay with my thoughts and planned for the day. I had to meet my grandmother's publishers; I had to visit the places she had visited, taking my mother with her. Yet again and again a feeling of futility knocked at the doors of my heart... I had to live out something, which would be in continuity with the lives of my mother, and especially that of my grandmother...but it also had to be my own... for it to be a true continuity...and I did not know what that was.

The police cars wailed insistently across the city...and the roses outside my window swayed in timeless moments each time I looked out, ... beckoning, communicating something I couldn't follow...I was sure.

The summer seemed to be disguising itself, wearing the cloak of autumn, and it began to drizzle.

The rain became insistent and cold, chasing away the warmth and brilliance of the days within the span of a night, and all the artists from the Place du Tertre as well. A ragged greyness hung about, making me glad of the smallness of my room. Making me glad too, of the presence of Madame Desmoulins and her family across the courtyard, because Fabrice was far away, on the other side of the town in his office at Saint-Germain-des-Prés, not realizing how cold and lonely this busy city of his was to a stranger.

I sat at my window, and watched the roses become drenched and sad in the rain. The leaves of the trees became heavy with gathering droplets and fell away a little, allowing a glimpse of the distant grey concreteness of the city to emerge occasionally from in between. I went to the kitchen to make myself another cup of tea, and saw the green slatted windows of Madame Desmoulins' upstairs rooms a little ajar, and my mind prickled with curiosity once more: who was *L'Ombre,* The Shadow? Who was the child calling in the quietness of the rooms occupied by the strange Dodi and his beautiful mother?

The phone trilled softly, but loud enough to be heard throughout the quiet of the rainy day. Fabrice, of course.

"What are you doing, *chérie*?" he asked gently.

"It's raining, Fabrice," I said

"Yes, darling, it's raining," he said in an amused voice. "So can I come up and we can have lunch at some small restaurant at Montmartre?"

My heart leapt with joy, so fed up was I of the solitude and the endless pittering of the rain on the leaves of the trees.

"Of course, Fabrice, that would be lovely!"

***

L'Esterel is a little place down at the Rue des Trois Freres, and I'd been there before once so I told Fabrice we could go there, and eat the day's specialty, whatever it was. He came in his diminutive car, but we left it up the hill parked outside my building, in spite of the rain, and walked down the steps and the winding streets to the restaurant, which is half-way below the level of the street, as the slope is steep where it is situated.

"I like that part about it," I said to Fabrice.

"It's nice to be with you, Mehjabeen, because I look at Paris with new eyes," he said, as though he really meant it.

As I sat with Fabrice sipping *menthe-â-l'eau,* as my grandmother might have done many years ago, I found myself totally at ease with the comforts that a bourgeois Parisian life offered. The waiter at L'Esterel is always half-shaven, or with a beard that never grows properly. You cannot imagine him but with his round tray in his hand, his big buck-teeth sticking out under his measly moustache, and his booming voice enticing clients, especially Americans. He speaks "*ay leetle eyngliche*" as do all restaurant and bar waiters these days, especially for tourists. He'll shake your hand, spin his tray, and move in a disjointed manner to reload the CD on the music deck. Often he sings along in a toneless croak, which pleases the customers. Everyone seems in a good mood when he is.

It was still drizzling when, replete with steak and salad, we walked back towards my apartment building. We took thc stairs part of the way, and Fabrice told me the prostitutes who used to stand there quite openly dressed in their peculiar manner, were no longer there, because the new Minister of the Interior, Sarkozy, had passed a law against prostitution, so now no one knew who was a sex-worker and who wasn't, and ordinary women were sometimes accosted. As we approached the Place du Tertre from behind the old church, we came upon a tall young man with a guitar, his head covered with a cloth bag, singing softly in the rain. A few passers by stopped to listen.

"I've made no promises," sang he,
"To these somnolent streets-
Just as the light flakes of the snow
Betray their whiteness at a touch
These slopes,
These crazy tilts
A tilted world,
Patches of colour all unfurled
At angles that you could never
I-ma-gine...!
The peaches and the cherries
In sum-merly crates
The doves cooing in the leafy glades,
All a function of these sleepy slopes...
Never chan-ging...
Never mov-ing...
And images upon them like a
Dé-coup-age....!

Where will I find my canvas?
Where will I hang my heart?"

"He's been here a long time, I guess," said Fabrice, smiling. "Knows all the seasons."

"He sounds American, doesn't he?" I ventured.

3
THE KINDNESS OF STRANGERS

A few mornings later, I awoke with the clear image of a painting in my head. A painting titled *"Meubles"*—"Furniture." There were blues and navies and violets, rectangles and open triangles. A painting I had seen somewhere? A Bracques? A Picasso? A Modigliani? Cubist? Expressionist? I could not place it. I could not return to the pleasant folds of sleep. When the morning light crept in through my half-open window, each object in my room silently reappeared from the sombre world of darkness; appeared bit by bit, then sat in the half-light as if by design put there, as if making a statement, as if addressing me.

And suddenly I knew the possibility of existing in two worlds, the real world and the image-world. Sharp and clear upon me, dawned this double experience. Were these the stirrings of creativity that shake so profoundly the inner world of a person that it appears at a parallel level with the outer world, the world of objective experience?

As the light grew brighter, and settled in patches over the objects in the room and the bedcover, and lit up the kitchen things, as the warbling of the birds announced the morning, as the newly warmed roses let off wafts of fragrance into the atmosphere, the world changed. It was filled with light and movement and sound, but it was still an inner world, an image world, and I realized that inside of me a door had opened, unexpectedly, allowing me the possibility of stepping into another dimension at a moment's notice, and that now, for all time I could alternate between the two almost at will.

A world where time could be slowed or accelerated, colours altered, sounds dimmed or accentuated, objects blurred or focused, a world that's a bit like the inverted world that comes in through a chink in your bathroom door, to sit upon the wall or floor; a patch, clear, and sometimes a mélange, a kaleidoscope, and then perhaps suddenly shadowed, as the breeze stirs the leaves in the trees outside.

I was elated at the discovery, but also troubled. Who could I talk to, about it? Not Daddy. Is this truly the alternate world of the Artist? Nerval's world? Dali's world? Or, am I going crazy? Have I inherited my mother's eccentricity? If so it could be called. Was the effect of opium, of absinthe, like this? A million questions rocked my thoughts. Would Fabrice understand? No, not with his Saint-Germain-des-Prés upbringing. Not with his Faubourg Saint-Honoré airs, with his Sixth Arondissement friends, not he!

What should I do? Paint more? Get an easel after all? I walked to the Rue des Norvins and looked up at the windows of Numero 22, the Folie Sandrin. What did Gérard de Nerval think about before he lost his mind? Could kindness and understanding cure Dodi? Then I walked to the Allée des Brouillards... deserted in the early morning rain and quiet; the Street of Mists...as it was called... and where Nerval had lived at one time. Nerval had been a poor poet and had no home, but went from apartment to apartment; Nerval, who lived in an inner world...and hanged himself ultimately. Inner worlds could be dangerous...one must beware of them. Like Nerval, one could get lost in them and never return. Yet, yet... to experience a double reality...!

Freedom, too, is an inner world to begin with, and does not exist externally, until you make it exist. So should one not seek freedom then, simply for fear of it?

It was cold yet, and I had eaten nothing, so I started walking back. I was troubled. The image-world must be honoured, but what could I paint that would be meaningful?

***

Madame Desmoulins smiled from behind the teapot. I was alone with her this time.

"His name is Jean-François, of course," she said, "but a friend of his father's nicknamed him Dodi." Madame Desmoulins was in a mood for confidences. Dodi's father had been a merchant, and he owned property in some parts of North Africa. Some of it had been ancestral, and he had bought it back not so long ago. Madame Desmoulins herself was of Italian descent, if one went back to the time of Marie de Medicis, she said. They had been happily married until Dodi was born, and apparently Monsieur Desmoulins had been so disappointed with the birth of a half-witted child that he went away and settled in his Algerian home in the small seaside town of Skikda. Madame Desmoulins had been left alone to cope with the emotional trauma of bringing up Dodi. Monsieur. Desmoulins sent money, lots of money, from time to time, he also visited once a year, but always went back despondent. He had a mistress or wife, and four other children in Skikda, and they probably gave him more pleasure with their warm ways than Dodi and his sophisticated mother. Several friends of Monsieur Desmoulins also visited time and again–Algerians, Moroccans, Tunisians–and one of them had insisted on calling little Jean-François Dodi, the Beloved, and the name had stuck.

Madame Desmoulins had a sister, Isabelle, who was married

to a lawmaker in the existing French Government. They were very well off and met with the highest placed officials in the Government. They frequented the Opera, saw ballets and plays at the Comédie Française, spent their summers in Monaco, weekends at La Baule, and shopped in London. Isabelle had three children, and she phoned every day, but social interaction with her sister was limited for obvious reasons. Not for lack of love nor of concern, but because of the position of her husband.

Isabelle was also involved in social work; she helped in the integration of immigrants, in small ways, gave large donations to causes, and often took on the wrath of her husband by going out of her way to help a refugee get a work permit, using her husband's connections.

"It was she," said Madame Desmoulins with barely veiled pride, "who helped me with Marina."

"Who's Marina?" I asked, intrigued.

"She's a refugee from Guatemala, and she has a child. They somehow came to France, deported from the United States, but now she has a home with me. I may not be able to do much, as my sister does, my circumstances being what they are, but at least if I help one person to live a decent life I shall give up the ghost without guilt."

I was struck by her candour, and the determination in the set of her chin. In all the people I had met in Fabrice's circle, in all the fine words they spoke, I had not encountered a single person who had the time to personally take on the troubles of another . In Paris people have such hectic lives they haven't a minute to spare, or they begin to believe they don't; in India, people may have a little time, but they are hampered by the rigid social hierarchy and by an unforgiving fatalism; it's all a question of belief, and Time bows to one's beliefs–smiling, mocking, changes like a djinn, taking any shape we choose to give it, knowing all the while that it is the Master, and we cannot defeat it, however we may try. Madame Desmoulins had found Time–the greatest gift one person can give another.

"Dodi calls her The Shadow, *L'Ombre*", Madame Desmoulins smiled again, "She is dark, darker than you. But I think she is beautiful, like you."

"Can I meet her? Does she speak English, or French?"

"A bit of both, and Spanish, if you know any."

***

As a little boy, Dodi went to the boys' Lycée at the foot of the steps leading up to the Sacré-Coeur. Within a few months the teachers realized that he would never learn as other children, and he was put in a special class that had children with learning problems. It was a heterogeneous group, and Dodi never really fitted in. He walked home up the Rue Foyatier, along the funicular, every afternoon, despondent and puzzled. The only thing that pleased him about going to school was the walk home, up the steps leading to the Sacré-Coeur, because he knew that as he mounted, his heart slowly lifted, and the closer he got to home the happier he felt. When he reached the main door of the building, his mood was at its best, and he was whistling. His mother believed he had had a good day at school, and after a while he began to believe it too. Hope being the most definite characteristic of human beings, besides Jealousy, the next day with renewed vigour, he went down the steps of the Rue Foyatier, with its tall trees throwing wilful shades over his descent. Thus passed Dodi's childhood, uneventfully, apart from the rare visits to his Tante Isabelle's where his cousins looked down their noses at him the moment their mother left them to themselves. Tante Isabelle was very kind indeed and always shed a few tears when they parted. Dodi could never understand the reason for so much emotion.

Madame Desmoulins must have been a lonely woman. There

were visits, she said, from friends of her husband, people he worked with, traded with. He sent them to see if his French family were doing well ... he sent them with money, always lots of money. There was Abdurrahman and his wife Najma who came once a year. There was Emir, who came more often, and Madame Desmoulins let drop that he had helped share her loneliness; it was he who started calling little Jean-François, Dodi. Emir stayed with the Desmoulins whenever he came to Paris. But his visits were rare now, as he had aged considerably in the past decade, said Madame Desmoulins, and was unable to travel so often. He was twenty years her senior. But Emir had been kind to her, very kind.

The kindness of strangers is a strange and lovely thing, as I too had discovered in this city where I knew no one, loved no one, and no one loved me. Of course I did not, even though young, believe that Fabrice loved me. Not for a moment could I bask in the luxury of such a thought, and I had always been a child without any need to prove my desirability, so much had I been loved by my parents, and so deeply had Rahul's love penetrated my being. But the kindness of strangers is what we live by–I learnt that. It is a warm cosy feeling to think that the world is full of kind strangers and you can address whomsoever you want without dread.

Madame Desmoulins, too, had experienced the kindness of a stranger, who had embraced her and her amorphous offspring with an unpredictable love, and brought fullness into a life left scorched like a twig in the desert sand, and to her, who was abandoned in her own land by her own people. And she, knowing the strangeness of kin, and the kindness of strangers, had in turn embraced The Shadow, the lost Guatemalan girl and her illegitimate child.

4
GRAETH

I don't know what it was about Graeth that first caught my fancy. He was tall and bony with a slightly asymmetrical face, a prominent nose, silvery blue eyes, and blonde hair parted at the side and cut in a blunt just below his ears. If you have a picture of the Pied Piper in your mind ...well, that was he. He had a crooked smile that made deep lines around his mouth, and a way of holding his head very straight and very slightly bent when he worked, that was rather appealing. Sometimes I thought he looked Transylvanian, because he wore a short cloak that added to the impression, but he was part Yugoslav, and lived in Denmark. And he was about thirty-five years old, rather ancient, from my point of view.

I met him outside Latifa Djemili's shop. I had dropped all my shopping just outside her door and was busy collecting it when I realized that I was blocking the path of two bony legs that wanted to enter the shop. It was late in the evening and the Rue Saint- Rustique was quite deserted.

La Rustique, as every artist who has ever come to Montmartre knows, is the only place to purchase your paints, pastels, brushes, canvases. It's a lovely, exciting shop, filled with intoxicating odours of oils and solvents and paper; it has a used palette signboard, and no name outside. It's just called after the little street where it finds itself, and everyone knows the small, bright Latifa Djemili who runs it, and she says she has a life where boredom isn't a word at all, because of all the stimulating people she gets to meet, thanks to her trade. Having a place right behind the Place du Tertre, where all the artists work, surely has only pluses!

Graeth helped me collect my scattered materials, and soon I found myself having coffee with him at the piano bar just beyond the Place du Tertre. It was funny, and I thought what Daddy would have said, to my sitting with a much older man at eight in the evening, drinking coffee. I do not know much about western music, but Graeth said they were playing Chopin. There were two pianists and one was black, and he played jazz after a while, which I recognized.

"You are a painter?" He wanted to know. "You are Indian? Ah, Art is ill-used in the world, ill-used! To project the wrong things, the wrong ideas. Art is a commodity, like love."

"Like love?" I wanted to know.

He did not answer immediately but tilted his head and gave me a penetrating look. Of course, did I not see how love was but a commodity?

The coffee tasted better than any coffee I had ever tasted. The notes of the piano seemed to enter my body and emerge from each pore, smoothly, and all his words about art and life seemed like everything I ever wanted to hear.

I should go, I thought. What will Daddy say? This man is a stranger, and an astute one. Europeans have different mores from us, he doesn't know what to expect from me. He may think I want something else, discussing love like this! He's not Fabrice, he's an older man, well over thirty! I got up quickly and made to pay for my coffee. He laid his hand on my arm, and said he would pay. He had nice hands. His fingers lingered on my arm, and I felt goose-bumps rising on my skin. I'm an idiot, I thought. Not emancipated enough, just an inexperienced Indian girl with very middle-class values. I must not bite off more than I can chew.

I said goodbye and he sat down again, glass in hand, smiled at me all the way as long as he could see me going down the road, the Rue des Norvins.

I thought a lot about Graeth the following week although I did not meet him even once. For some reason, I wanted to discuss my thoughts about the inner eye of the artist with him … the double world in which I believed it was possible to exist; I felt he would understand. There are certain things you feel certain about when you are young; I was sure he would enlighten me further along this path.

I was yet to learn perhaps that somctimcs communication at the intellectual level is not enough for life, ...that love and communication can be two different things altogether, …that a person may not represent at the level of lived experience the same he may at the level of the imagined, … and that each relationship is important to one's development.

Fabrice thought I should behave young, and I too wanted to grow younger in my heart once more, for one cannot carry sorrow around forever. But if you look into the eyes of the Parisians, you know even the young are ancient in a way, the steadiness and communication in their gaze is the age which is the bequest of a preserved culture, and everyone who lives there for even a small while absorbs that *ancience*, that knowingness, and even I, with my mind sponge-like, my transcultural being, flitting like a ghost across the walls created by social hierarchies, had soaked in that *ancience* in little time, and it was so new that I could feel it in every pore, in every movement, and it strengthened me, yet detached me from my own self, because it was making me become what I was not, but someone more layered, in a way more whole, someone unlike anyone.

***

Life falls around one like a pack of flash cards, and it is rare that one should see in it linearity, a logical linkage, or even a chronological unfolding. My life, after my meeting with Dodi seemed to take on an accelerated and illogical aspect, carrying me forward from day to day with a speed I could not control. What had he foreseen that his mother and I had been unable to? The question crawled about in my mind like an insidious worm, a fine one, albeit, a very fine one, like a filament, like a string, floating about, weightless, irrational. I seemed to have lost the thread of my own thoughts, the reason for my visit to Paris, the reason of my being at all; it was as if the ground was shifting beneath my feet at a speed that was not in accord with the speed of my steps.

I sat down in my room and drew Montmartre as an ice-cream cone with many wafers stuck in it, each wafer had a face on it–Graeth, Dodi, Madame Desmoulins, Manès Trigot, Marina, myself, Dominique, the Polish woman who opened the door at the Poste, shadowy faces floated in the background–Emir, Nadjma–people whom I did not know, but nowhere was there a wafer for Fabrice–poor Fabrice who was my only support, the only real person in this whole topsy-turvy world, he had no wafer in my ice-cream!

***

Then one day I met Manès in the Metro.

I was walking around in the Luxembourg gardens, ...a bit lost, a bit lonely, and the rain had emptied it temporarily of all sane humans, the odd *clochard* still hanging about on the green chairs, drunk, impervious to the fine droplets that slowly drenched everything, I knew what Sartre meant when he said that the sad thing about human beings is that they feel like extras in the world. I think rainy Paris does give you that feeling, everyone is extra in relation to the world, "*de trop*". The trees too droop, and feel "*de trop*", but it is only people like Dodi who are considered extra by others, except his mother, who values his unformed being, his meaningless life; but then, is not all life meaningless? Many were the people there that I could see as extras in relation to the life that Fabrice led. And the woman with the cigarette and the many words...who snatched the words of others and built of them new sentences that meant something else....With such thoughts confused, I could no longer bear the loneliness and decided to descend into the depths of the metro and head back tor Montmartre, crossing Barbès-Rochechouart, getting off at Anvers and walking all the way up, or I could take the funicular.

I met Manès Trigot in the metro.

I did not take the empty seat next to him, as we were not really even acquaintances. A nod, a tight smile; what more could we exchange?

A group of teenagers was creating a ruckus near the door, squabbling and mocking like a group of mynahs in a puddle. Just as the train was leaving Châtelet, three of the teenagers forced the doors open and pushed one of their companions out. I gasped, fearing the worst, but they were probably well versed with such risks, and they laughed as the third boy stood waving his fist at them from the platform. A Frenchman sitting next to me looked up from his paper at my gasp, and catching his eye, I said, "They could've killed themselves!"

"It would be of the least interest to me, mademoiselle, if they had," he replied sardonically, "The least."

"Would have served them right, in fact," I heard Manès Trigot from the other side, his high voice very loud, very convinced.

I turned to see if I had been mistaken about the teens - were they not schoolboys, but criminals? No, indeed they were between fifteen and seventeen, but they were mostly Arabs, North Africans, but Parisian, very much so.

I turned to Manès Trigot, "You think they don't have families? Mothers, who might be waiting anxiously for their return?"

"Mademoiselle, *quelle idee*!"What an idea!–he replied, looking very morose, his hands swivelling comically at the wrists, his pale blue eyes distressed. "When they do not think of their mothers, why should we?" He appeared to have suffered some personal injury by my mention of their mothers. I deemed it better to hold my peace, and turned my attention to the darkness whizzing by until the train reached the Gare Du Nord. For the man beside me and Manès, these boys were *de trop*; they did not have a right to be there.

***

I went home and again the next morning the same thoughts came to my mind. What was I going to do with my day? What would I learn? And the morning, sometimes aimlessly, became afternoon, then evening ….

It had to go on in that very way. There was a hill and it was like a top wound over with string; the streets. An evening with Graeth, and an evening with Fabrice; I was a woman with choices. Yet what preoccupied my mind was the moist dusk of early summer descending over the windows of Madame Desmoulins' home, windows lit with a yellow glow in the interiors. There sat two men of different ages, the snail and the angel, doing math. On the top floor the Shadow kept her young one warm by the fireplace. And the lady with the fine nose and eyes with the memories of two men, the disappointed escapee husband, and the old and no longer able lover; the woman all alone in the kitchen hoping against hope that the boy who was not all there would have a future of some kind.

Leaves blown about by the wind littered the pavements as scarves flowed over it and heels clicked busily across. The summer seems to have gone home to the east, and the south, and left nothing but imagination behind. An imaginary world, so far from real that it creates a reality more concrete than the natural.

Should I knock at Madame Desmoulins door, or should I answer Fabrice's SMS on my cell? An evening at the Flore, with wine and cheese and *pâté de foie gras* and tomato salad with olive oil and parsley, and music, and quiet, urgent voices chattering into the cold night … how tempting!

I knock at the darkened door. Madame Desmoulins' face lights up and she smiles at me. We go directly into the kitchen, quietly. I nod and smile shortly at the two men, not wishing to disturb them.

There is a smell of Pril and I can see a few cups washed and dried on the table. A loaf of *pain de campagne* lies cut on the sideboard.

This time it is coffee. Moroccan. I express the hope of meeting the Shadow. Perhaps when Manès Trigot leaves and Dodi goes to drop him to the metro station, Les Abbesses, then she will call down Marina.

5
The Bereavement of Agnès Desmoulins

I began the new oil painting after Emir died. The only friend that Madame Desmoulins ever had. A ship, a liner, sunk in the Red Sea, the Al-Salaam; eight hundred dead, maybe more. And old Emir, returning from Haj, among them. He had planned to go to Cairo, where he had had a business once, and where his eldest son still worked. But the forces of the Red Sea had planned other things. The deep hidden dragons of tragedy emerged, breathing fire; and water and sky and flame became one. Emir was gone forever.

Madame Desmoulins' salon looked like an unrestored medieval tableau, so thick was the gloom that filled it, so still and unmoving sat the mourners, so fixed and lightless their eyes appeared. Dodi, nebulous Dodi, his arm hung over the sofa, in a black T-shirt. Madame Desmoulins, a widow who could not mourn. Manès Trigot, a meaningless, transparent being in the tragedy, comically clutching a math book. A baby's intransigent wail, a mother's hushing voice, soothing, a backdrop, unseen presences in the tableau. Isabelle, distraught, knowing not how to comfort her sister in an unacknowledged loss.

Isabelle's arrogant offspring, upper-class *lycéens*, soft-faced, uncommunicative, untouched by their surroundings. The cold rain pattering on the fogged panes.

I went back to my apartment and unpacked my good canvas. I unrolled it and carefully fitted it onto my new easel. The time had come, and I began to paint. Of the unseen narrative nature of the visual. Through colour and light and shadow I would attempt to build it into a living instant, an instant prepared at any moment to move backwards or forwards in Time, and become another. The metamorphosal character of emotion once captured would infinitely appeal to the perceiving eye, suddenly once, and then forever; responding in seamless perfection to the transformatory quality of experience.

The painting christened itself *The Bereavement of Agnès Desmoulins*. It reminded me, for some reason, of Manet's *Olympe*, in its contrasts of light and shade. In the background appeared a dark Arab man in a white djellaba, holding a baby. Next to him, a tall black African, perhaps Nubian, wearing a leopard skin draped around his shoulders, a grey turban, and carrying a tall spear. Unrealistic figures, speaking of the travelling soul of Agnès Desmoulins, of Humankind.

In the unseen there was the sea. Tall, white buildings with large windows, letting the sea into Agnès Desmoulins' soul, as she stood, young, on a balcony, facing the blue. The sea that brought him to her, the sea that took Emir away.

A bleak wind whipped around the curling streets of Montmartre, and when I went to the post office, a few days later, I stopped by the Tunisian's store to buy some cheese and bread. I saw Madame Desmoulins emerge from the heavy studded doorway of the church Saint-Jean at the Abbesses. She said she had started going there after Emir's death. I noticed she called Dodi Jean-François sometimes, too. Perhaps, her being, spread thin too long across countries was trying to withdraw, like an amoeba, into the confines of a single city, and assume a shape, an identity not required heretofore. I knew that, yet I knew too, that the sea would not let her go; it would enter forever, even on the windy, drizzly, grey days of Montmartre, blue and green, through white, sunny windows, reclaiming her interest, her regard, across which it had voyaged so long, towards Monsieur Desmoulins, and his other family, with sorrow; towards Emir and his love, with longing.

It's important to be recognized as someone …it's important for people to be able to identify one, for accordingly do they give you a status, accordingly they need to put you in a slot—that way interaction becomes easier, and one feels less threatened by the unknown. Yet, it seemed, the unknown would always be a part of Agnès Desmoulins, a part she must hide, put away, and continue….

***

The next day, I dressed, ate a small breakfast of coffee and croissant, went over to the painting, perused it for a few moments, added a stroke here and there according to my mood and inspiration, then locked my door and went down. As usual, I met Dodi in the street, walking his bicycle, wearing a warm muffler and cap, his face screwed up against the wind. Seeing me, he stopped, and gave me a blank but concentrated look.

"I know you have seen them. They have come, they are there, I have seen them, and I know you have seen them too."

"Who?" I asked, slightly frightened. Was he talking about Marina and her baby?

"The ones who have crossed the *Méditerranée*, the troubled ones. The ones who speak different tongues. You saw they were there when Tante Isabelle came."

Now I was terrified. Feigning coolness, I murmured, "*Oui, oui,*", and quickly walked away, nodding amicably to Dodi. I do not know how long he stood there, looking after me.

***

As the sunshine slipped in and out of the oddly darkened days, a momentary visitor, the cafés grew brighter and fuller, more enticing, creating worlds within, full of luminosity and laughter; and the Seine greyed, like an old woman, her surface become wrinkled in the wind, and flecked with white. "What kind of summer was this?" said the people in the streets.

And all through the noise and the cold, the world inside, the Other World, crept upon the pavements, almost an intruder, and claimed bits of reality for itself, for its images, putting them away in its large overcoat, each with a surreptitious glance, to see if it were being watched–...but no, no one could see, so lost were they, each in his own capsule of joy or sorrow, love or longing, hope or despair.

The broken teacup fell in my lot one rainy afternoon. After we had travelled many days and nights on the waves that followed Emir's sudden departure from Agnès Desmoulins' life. She took my hand over the spotty table cloth, for her an expansive gesture: "Mehjabeen" (she pronounced it *Meyjumbee*), "You are a kind girl," she said . "I should have been born in a sunny land, or at least in the South."

"There are lands," she continued, "dark and lonely, Mehjabeen, where the soul lives. They are not bright and rich and merry as is Paris. There are no operas, no cinemas, no cafés. There are deserts and vast lands, and people with quiet faces. So Emir told me. Where they speak not of how they live and what they experience within, there the soul lives, in silence."

I thought of the untended yellow stretches of Rahimganj, of the quiet-eyed children playing in the dust, of their white smiles, and a pang assailed me. Goose pimples stood out on my skin.

"You are kind, and warm, like the people of sunny lands."

I was about to contradict her, to say that in my country too, people could be callous, crude and brutal, but something stopped me, not patriotic fervour, but the wish to not shatter the careful image of other lands she had constructed, and wanted to live by. Because she felt more akin to strangers, than to her own countrymen.

***

In the late afternoon I was still restless, Bernardo and Anita were nowhere to be seen, and I had still not been introduced to the Shadow, who I was longing to see. Fabrice had called, but for some reason I did not want to call him back. He spent a lot of money on me, and that, somewhere, made me uncomfortable.

It was still light despite the clouds, so I walked down the hill, sometimes taking the stairs, two by two, ... to the bus top right at the bottom on the main road, and went to Boulevard Saint-Michel for a stroll.

Graeth was very fond of Greek sandwiches and I was glad to meet him at the Place Saint-Michel where he sat propped against his *moto,* eating a sandwich, and making a sketchy picture of the café facing the Seine.

"*Hola*!" said his Spanish companion to me. He was a curly-haired young man with a merry smile. I never saw him before or after. Graeth had a twinkle in his eye as he looked at me.

"Love is bartered and sold, as is Art and Talent," he said, but without bitterness this time. The wind was whipping his golden hair around his craggy face and he looked more like the Pied Piper than ever, leading the children down to the River Weser.

I bought myself some *frites*, and we went and stood on the bridge across the square, the Pont Saint-Michel, looking down at the Seine. The wind played with the leaves, and with the scarves of the *bouquinistes* even carrying their caps away at times. The Spaniard with the unruly hair left, and Graeth moved closer to me until our arms touched. I munched my fries, and waited for him to speak. His eyes had held that communicative twinkle ever since we had met.

"You have freckles," he said in an amused tone.

"Unfortunately," I said dryly

"And your hair's not an even colour either."

"I'm a bit like my grandmother. Her mother was English. I've got the worst of both sides."

"No, I wouldn't say that," he said, very nicely, "You have that dark Indian empathy in your eyes, the beauty painters cannot catch."

"If you say so," I replied lightly.

Suddenly Graeth turned and grabbed my arm, the twinkle still in his eye. His grip was firm and strangely comforting. Then his arm went about my waist and his lips were on mine. One large hand cupped my breast and I felt my breath leave my body. All through the kiss I thought of Joffrey de Peyrac, the lame Duc of Languedoc kissing Angélique for the first time. She had not known a kiss could be so sweet. It was over as promptly as it had begun, and I felt it had happened to someone else. Not to Javed's daughter Mehjabeen. I'd been kissed by the River Weser, by the Pied Piper of Hamelin. Maybe I'd been inviting it. I continued eating my *frites*, not moving away, not wanting to appear gauche. Perhaps *Meyjumbee* had been kissed.

Some things happen, and they don't. Some things don't happen, and they do. Reality is elusive, optional.

***

The designs on the raiment of the figures became more intricate as I worked on them. Cutwork on the fringes. The shadows spoke more deeply, purple and green and grey. The faces were plainer by comparison, still almost expressionless, as if waiting...to develop into someone...

I became afraid of my own work. I dragged the canvas into the sitting room, farther away from my bedroom. It frightened me at night. Who were the unknown mourners at *The Bereavement of Agnès Desmoulins*? And Dodi had seen them too. Something was compelling me to create a world I had no connection with. To which I did not belong. To connect to people I did not know. Some things happen and do not. Some things don't happen, and do. Art was teaching me the path to optional realities with which we live every day, making choices, yet never analyzing the process. And from moment to moment we pick from the pack of realities, a card, sometimes of our liking, from an open pack, sometimes a blind card, and call it Destiny.

***

Anita and Bernardo lounged with their coffees on the wooden chairs near the piano bar and we sat with our scarves and coats outside. Latifa Djemili was passing by and she joined us. Abdurraheim, the Algerian bartender smiled at me conspiratorially, Graeth threw me a Joffrey de Peyrac look from time to time.

"I hate the Americans!" said Bernardo suddenly. "They have too much. They think they own the earth."

"They do," said Graeth darkly. "They buy our art. We need them."

"And we give them ingratiating smiles for the money," Anita looked troubled.

Abdurraheim brought hot croissants with our coffee. "A lot of people who come here say they hate Arabs."

"Of course they do," said Latifa, "But not all."

"I live in Aubervilliers," said Abdurraheim, "My eighteen-year-old son was arrested for something he didn't do, and they kept him for ten days in the lock-up. I've been thirty-five years in France, and he was born here."

There was a silence, heavy, like a purple rain cloud.

Graeth looked dark again. "I'm leaving soon. Paris is bursting with unhappened things that are bound to happen."

"But Art will survive," said Latifa brightly, "Art survives everything. That's what Dali thought too."

Abdurraheim was still hovering around, emboldened by my presence, and Latifa's.

"They've robbed all the museums in Baghdad and the Art will surface in museums in the West a few decades from now. The white man is a robber, of oil as well as Art."

Anita smiled suddenly at Abdurraheim. "*Allez,*" she said kindly, defusing the pause. Then she turned to me, "How is your secret painting coming along?"

"Well, I suppose," I said hesitantly.

Bernardo slapped my shoulder in an avuncular fashion, "Mehjabeen is making a figurative painting when all the young contemporary artists are embracing the abstract and the symbolic."

"There was an exhibition of Tantric art at the Beaux Arts recently," said Anita, munching her croissant vigorously.

Bernardo guffawed, his moustaches drenched at the edges in his coffee.

"Why are you laughing?" asked Anita, looking at him with a proprietary indignation, as only a wife can at a husband. "You put too much kahlua in your coffee."

"At Mehjabeen, *cara*!" said Bernardo, still shaking with laughter. "Imagine her, and Tantric art!"

"I don't pretend to understand it," I said in my defence, "But I do feel that ... well ... like in my painting, for example, the shadows and the designs, the embellishments, speak more than the figures or faces.I can't say why. Why can't the figurative be symbolic as well?"

I sat and contemplated Bernardo's nose turning red. Optional existences; Life, a series of optional tableaux. Sometimes our tableaux are filled with the inessential, with intruders. Things which are not happening. If only there could be an exchange of images between different works of art, like it happened at Hogwarts School, where figures could flit from painting to painting, to interact with those inhabiting others! Then one could actually search for the essential. The rich warm moments of living. I asked Anita what she thought, afraid Bernardo or Graeth might mock me.

"Yes," she said, "like the Americans are essential at one level; but the rich, warm feeling is missing when you are with them."

"That's a terrible generalization, *cara*," admonished Bernardo. "I had an American girlfriend once.'

Anita looked daggers at him, but that was all.

***

I spoke to my father that night. He said I couldn't drift endlessly in Montmartre, and that I should see my grandmother's friends and publishers more often, and Fabrice, if I really wanted. Then I must return to India at the earliest. It wasn't the money, he said, he was missing me.

I did not tell him that I had only yet discovered some of the pieces of the jigsaw and putting them together was something I wanted to do. Could I leave without discovering why my painting was developing in the direction it was? Could I tell him I still had to meet The Shadow? My father is a good man. Intelligent, down to earth, pragmatic. He let me go at so young an age because of his guilt over my mother. She had longed for another life, and he had expected her to be happy in his small-town-mango-orchard-newspaper-editor existence. By not forcing me to stay, he was, in a way, making it up to her. He loved her, even now, I knew. But men often think they know what is best for women, and that's a serious mistake. They want to mould them, and guide them, in everything. It's a kind of denial of their reality. And emancipated women are considered worthy only if they "walk shoulder-to-shoulder" with men.

That is why alternate realities needed to come into play. To Zehra Phuphi, my aunt, the interior was an alternate existence, in which she could sew and embroider, have her hair oiled and hennaed by old Qamrun Bua, pickle fruit and vegetables, and feel she had some control over her life. In these interiors men were but visitors, invitees, their powers magically diminished as they entered.

Yet in my mother's family, interiors had little place in a woman's life. I am like that too—we have to live and experience the external world as well, participate in it, and not be "put away". But it seems in this external world, as soon as they step out, women lose their powers.

I haven't told Daddy that I'm keen to know what being a woman means here, in the developed world. Are they too, allowed only a partial existence, as are most women in India?

Could I tell him that *The Bereavement of Agnès Desmoulins* stood by my window day after day?

I wove into it the small soft shadows of the morning, the warm angles of occasional sunshine, the angular darknesses of the night ... I knew there was much more, and perhaps another figure, and another, that must complete the tableau. The intricacy of some areas, like the turban of the Nubian, was in sharp contrast to the rough patches of paint that lit up the window by which he stood. I knew I had to complete the painting, then I could leave Paris.

***

I was with Fabrice at a *soirée* a few evenings later, at the Faubourg Saint-Honoré. Among the chic women was the glamorous Diane de Selliers, tall and blonde and large-boned, discussing with admirers her wonderful books combining art and poetry, and talking about her young son. But I was lost in this world. Fabrice kept me close by his side, and asked me once or twice why I looked pale.

"You're not drinking our wonderful wine!" the gracious host took my arm and led me to the bar, where he poured me a red wine, not too dry, he said, not too sweet. "You must try it," he said, leading me back to Fabrice. Fabrice was in conversation with some polished-looking men and women I hadn't yet met.

"And what do you think of the French, *petit oiseau de l'Inde?*" asked a chivalrous middle-aged man, calling me "little bird of India", while his wife looked coldly at me with glittering green eyes that matched the emeralds and white sapphires around her long, slim neck.

I took a gulp of the wine. I felt the warmth trickle down my chest and spread to my arms and stomach. Such people made me nervous.

"Oh, I love the French!" I said. "So polite, so *gentil,* it's a pleasure. So aware, so well-read, so poetic! It's a wonderful experience to be among them!"

"And isn't Paris the most beautiful city in the world?" someone else was asking me. Fabrice was smiling kindly at me, proudly. His sophisticated friends were taking interest in his Indian companion.

My throat felt dry and I took another gulp of the wine. It tasted better than before. I emptied the glass. A pleasurable sensation of well-being entered my limbs along with the earlier warmth. I even felt confident enough to respond in French.

"*Un accent parfait!*" said the green-eyed woman. A perfect accent.

I thought of Graeth. I saw in my mind, his eyes; one blue, one slightly green.

"Paris is indeed beautiful," I was saying, and I knew Graeth was talking inside my head. "But like a lovely prostitute."

A small silence, and they waited for me to continue. Always *poli.*

"Decked out with her wares to entice the dollar-laden tourist. She smiles like a *prostituée* if your pocket is full. She grimaces if it is empty. She is for sale." My voice became smaller, but more incisive. I was speaking for effect, and I wasn't afraid anymore. "Sarkozy may have officially banned prostitution but Paris has lost it soul, I think: it has been bought."

The host smiled equably, "I suppose you can say the same about Rome or Venice …"

"I have not been there," I said.

The Pied Piper smiled inside me.

The green-eyed woman said, "It's only in the summer months, when the Parisians go away anyway. And then, Paris is now so full of *étrangers.*" She was definitely far right. "So many ethnically different people here now. More than a fifth."

I decided to take her on. The Pied Piper was on my side. "I love the French culture and the people, but they continue to be very colonial."

A silence again. I looked pointedly at the green-eyed lady. She was my principal adversary.

"I see all the menial jobs and the small jobs being done by North Africans. Or even the Poles. They seem to be employed in all the occupations the French wouldn't want to do. First they were colonized in their own land. Now they are doubly colonized here. The whites remain the masters. The others are holding up the entire system, constituting the lower rungs, agreeing to live in conditions the French wouldn't dream of."

Fabrice was looking at me in surprise. It didn't matter if I lost him, I thought wildly. I was telling a difficult truth, and no one could deny it.

"Well," said my adversary, her mouth thinning, "You have had the caste system in your own country for centuries." The French know everything, unlike the Americans.

"If the discussion were about my country I would not be so quick to deny it," I said boldly. "But I thought we were talking about Paris."

"The pot can't call the kettle black," she said, a harsh note in her cultured voice.

"One wrong does not mitigate another, Madame," I countered coolly. "I am in your country, which is a developed nation, a nation that has given the world ideas and ideals. Liberty, Equality and Fraternity. Yet if you care to walk down the Boulevard the Rochechouart, or the Boulevard Barbès, you will know what I mean. I live in the eighteenth, in Monsieur Houllebecq's apartment."

"*Ah, le mystérieux Monsieur Houllebecq!*" she cried rapturously and the topic was changed. She was more sophisticated than I had imagined.

The evening brightened again and I danced with Fabrice, evading his teasing, pretending, smiling, a little high on the wine –play-acting is such an exciting part of human social life, it gives dimensions to dull moments, magnitude to empty hours, hidden spaces to vacant encounters, like labyrinthine temples with small unostentatious facades.

I could even dream of inviting Diane de Selliers to see my painting, *The Bereavement of Agnès Desmoulins.*

***

When I was saying goodbye to Fabrice, he said gently, "You're taking it too hard."

"I'm sorry for my outburst with your friends," I said, "I stroll down Barbès and Rochechouart, Fabrice. And also down the Rue des Martyrs right up to the Opera. I can't help noticing the differences. I'm sorry."

Again I said nothing about Agnès Desmoulins and her life.

***

I woke up suddenly at twelve that night, and couldn't go back to sleep, so made myself a cup of coffee. I went over to my painting and stared long and hard at *The Bereavement*.... Then I mixed some paint and changed the eyes of the Nubian, to one green, one blue. I finished my coffee, and jumped back in bed with a strange satisfaction undulating within my breast.

After that, however, I had to cover the painting when I was not working on it. The pied eyes of the Piper seemed to be looking around, at every corner of the room, at all the movements I made, and although I knew it was silly, ridiculous, I stuck a large sheet of newspaper over the picture, like a veil, which I could lift off to work if I wanted.

6
Grenoble

I had told Fabrice that I intended to go to Grenoble to look for any leads that I could find to my mother's childhood friend, Zamurrad. I had tried the yellow pages, and everything else that I could, but it seemed there was no such person in Grenoble.

Fabrice, kind as always, said he would take me there, and if we liked we could go by train as driving in his car might take too long. I called Daddy and asked him if it was okay for me to go with Fabrice, and he was only too happy, because he was thinking of my safety first.

So one morning, Fabrice called to say that he was free to go now and we could be there over the weekend and one extra day in the week, to be able to go to visit the offices if required. For it was unlikely the offices would be open over the weekend. I was terribly grateful to him, of course, but a little afraid. He had said earlier that he would accompany me to London once Qadeer Mamoon returned, but that so far had been a possibility in the not-so-near future and I hadn't given the practical aspects of it much thought.

We took the train the following morning, and, funnily, Fabrice slept most of the way. This gave me ample time to think about my search, where it would lead me, and what exact satisfaction I was seeking. Since my dream about the painting, life had changed. Life changed then on from day to day. I had the feeling I was not at the wheel. Whom I met, who remembered me from another time, like Dodi, perhaps, was not in my hands. I had not asked for all of this. All I wanted was to know for a bit why my mother had suffered so, but the answer lay not here, it lay not in the external reality but in internal and eternal truths, if in today's world we believe in their existence at all anymore. Some thing was dragging me, a kind of magnetic force that told me this world was not mine, that somewhere lay an unfinished story, that some parts of me were unformed, that they were still sticking to the egg-shell—I was indeed not free. Freedom is accorded to goats, like the goat of Monsieur Séguin, freedom that leads into the mouth of the wolf; no, I was not free.

It was late when we arrived, and we checked into a tall modern hotel by the highway. We went back to the main town, strolled around the Place Grenette, the old town square, found a McDonald's where we ate a burger each, as we'd feasted on chocolates on the train, and weren't too hungry. Fabrice was unusually quiet, and I was too busy trying to sort out my own feelings to make much conversation. Would I find my mother's friend? What was the probability of meeting her at all? Did Fabrice consider me foolish? After all, we'd checked the yellow pages, enquired at the police stations, everything. But wasn't it Fabrice himself who said that the French were careless in many matters? lost people were their specialty, he'd said. And if in fact I *did*, by some chance, manage to locate her, how would she receive me?

We said goodnight, back at the hotel, and I slept fitfully in the small cold room on the seventh floor. I could see the highway from my window if I looked out, and the trucks passing on it all night long.

The next morning was bright and warm, and we took a tram

to the main town again. The squares of the old town were brightly decorated with buntings, and milling with students and tourists. There was a magician by the fountain of the Place de Metz, and a band of American Indians in traditional dresses played deep haunting tunes on cedar and bamboo flutes. We stood and watched for a while, then walked towards the river, the Isère. Fabrice was still uncommunicative, and I wondered if he was thinking me daft, or, was he just humouring me, indulging me, as one would a child. Was there anything more I wanted from him? I wondered.

The ancient houses crouched close to each other and to the river, separated from it by a mere path at times. We crossed over from the dingy Pont Marius to the left bank, and sat under the trees there. I left Fabrice sitting on the bench and walked down the grassy bank from where I could see the Alps, the silent, unrevealing flow of the Isère, ... a soundless image of continuity, of timelessness, in the backdrop of the bony, knuckled Alps, now bare, the fourth century tower of the castle, grey and black topped, like a cement joker, the castle of the imprisoned princess Zamurrad. ... only the Isère offered freedom, offered journeying, escape, tenderness. Tenderness is the beckoning to liberty. Monsieur Séguin's goat but had to climb the mountain to be devoured by the wolf, her liberator. What Monsieur Séguin could not offer was the tenderness of freedom.

The Isère is a river, with the depth and swiftness of thought, with an apparent quietude of being, with a dark side, and the side filled with reflections:the Alps, the spire, the téléphérique leading up to the fortress, the Bastille, made for the war.If one were to compare, the Alps are mountains, large, beautiful, but not mysterious as the Himalayas, not unattainable. And the Isère has not been "managed", like the Seine in Paris, its wildness is still there beneath the reflections, its feral nature heard in its quiet singing, in its constant caress of its harsh yellow and brown stone banks. In the great flood of 1859 it had spread its tentacles all over Grenoble, and there were no banks, no quays in those days to restrain her flow. The quays contain her wildness now, but only a little, you can sense it in the hypnotic flow through the town if you look for a moment without averting your gaze.

As I stood there, I felt strangely inhabited by the undulating nature of existence; it could buffet me, and cradle me, and swing and sway me with itself. The nebulous nature of the earth responding to the throbbing of an outer universe, the prominences of the sun, the craters of the moon, the seas of Serenity and Tranquillity, and the beneficence of reflected light. Yes, there were things that happened to us that were not within our control.

On the other side of the river from the castle is the underbelly of the town, where the immigrants and the refugees live. I asked Fabrice if it were safe for me to walk alone around these quarters — he had friends at the university he wanted to visit, and an author of science fiction who was very keen to see him. He said I should keep my cell phone on, and not go into dark alleyways, and I should be okay. So we parted for the day, planning to meet in the evening at the Place de Metz, by the fountain in front of the book shop.

It was strange, actually, quite coincidental, how I was able to get information about Lise. There are parks along the river bank, and then the streets and the grimy buildings are a little below the parks and the bank; they were deserted at that time of day, around two in the afternoon, and I was a little afraid to get lost. I found there were hardly any squares, no touristy trappings, no pretty *café terrasses* with blue and maroon awnings; it was indeed a dull dingy quarter, it was an area where mostly workers lived, and they all seemed to have gone to work. A few old women peeped from narrow balconies, some with black scarves and skirts; I thought perhaps Lise would peep out too, and I wouldn't recognize her of course.

A dark, curly haired woman in her forties was sweeping the

front of a bistrot. Could it have been Zamurrad?

It was almost five. I was strolling along in the street approximately behind the ancient convent which housed the Dauphines museum; suddenly a man of about sixty, walking from the other direction, who was the only other person in the lane, beamed at me. I smiled back tentatively.

"*Qu'est-ce que vous cherchez?*" he asked me. What was I looking for? Was it so apparent? He said he was as old as the convent, which would be about four hundred years; he was joking of course. Drawn by his amicability, I decided to tell him my story, strange though it was....

The man who claimed to be as ancient as the convent said, yes, there had been a woman there, by the name of Eméraude, a Moroccan woman, a nurse, they called her the Russian Arab, because she had a Russian surname and a Russian mother. This Eméraude owned a small boat, in which she used to go out on weekends down the river. She worked at the Centre Médico-Psychologique for children and adolescents at the Place des Géants.

Then when the old Russian lady was no more, and Eméraude was alone, she would go sailing oftener. She left one day, four or five years ago, in her boat down the river and no one ever saw her again. It had been a big story in the local tabloids: they located the boat, but her body was never found.

The castle belongs to the fourth century and the square is full of musicians, the water in the fountain reflects the bookshop. Fabrice says it's a story; that he does not believe the lady went off in a boat. I know, I know deep inside that it is true. Fabrice does not remember or maybe I never told him – my mother took Roy's boat and went away down the Gomti River, never to be seen again. The same time as the story of the Russian-Arab nurse with the curly hair.

We found the number of the hospital, and after many calls made by poor Fabrice, who didn't believe in the story anyway, they told him , that yes, a nurse of that name had worked there some years ago. I was vindicated, but still Fabrice continued to question the evidence—it may be another person, how could we be sure? I argued how many people of that name existed, who were Moroccans and had Russian mothers? But whether he believed it or not, my heart was at rest. That was the way it had to be. My mother had never been alone, and that comforted my spirit.

The tram wove its way around the town, and then we got off and saw the city museum. At the bookshop under the hotel room, I met Tatiana. At first she was very reserved. But I had gone there every time I passed by and soon our Asian-ness seemed to strike chords somewhere.

When the Soviet Union broke up, the Press in India told us nothing of what went on inside the independent republics. What happened to their people, what happened to their cultures, their languages, their political set-ups? What happened to their families, their schools, their libraries, their jobs, their way of life? Had we nothing at all to learn from those? Are we so far removed from another people that we care not an iota what happens to them as long as their lives apparently seem not to affect ours?

Tatiana Dmitrieva's daughter married a Welsh boy and went away to Wales. They had met at the University of Grenoble. Her son Misha had a French wife. The two grandchildren were French, and knew no Russian at all. Of course they were all French now. France had become their homeland because Russia had not allowed them a life, the kind of life to which they had been brought up, as Soviet Russians. Speaking the same tongue, leading a common life ... when the Republics broke away, each of them wanted a distinct identity, and in that they could not accept people from other republics who had different mores; what could a couple like Tatiana and Dmitri do? They belonged to different countries now, and each was being chased away by the other's kingdom! How much hatred is there in the hearts of human beings, who until yesterday lived together, suddenly turn on each other? Upon hearing Tatiana's story I looked away - had not the Partition of India shown to perfection this side of human nature? Had not the riots in Delhi after the assassination of Indira Gandhi revealed the same? Had not the riots in Gujarat, the Nellie massacre, unveiled this beast within us?

And then, there is no redressal, no post-trauma justice. Each crime is heaped upon the last, and the ghosts of each continue to haunt us forever. They haunt the earth, fly about, screaming in anger and hate, uncontained in time or space, released for an eternity ... but then, what is an eternity? A split-second in the life of the earth? And in each moment of suffering the human heart lives that eternity. Oh Fabrice, if only you knew how I know that Eméraude was Zamurrad and she went away on a boat and was never seen again.

"Your grandmother was a poet? Died young? In Paris? Ah! The stories of poets are sad, sad indeed. In the nineteen thirties the poets who came away from Soviet Russia met a similar fate, Poplavsky and his friend died of a drug overdose, they said they "left for the land of sleep." But does sleep bring peace always? What if one is haunted by nightmares? Past traumas? Nicholas Gronsky fell in the subway and came under a train, at the Station Pasteur." I did not know the stories of the poets Tatiana spoke of. But it made me sad, to hear they had suffered. She was right; poets had a sad life, even in freedom.

Why does each of us have a life all of one's own, so different from all the rest? Is it really necessary in the Great Plan of Things, or, are the differences negligible in His eyes? Or, in the eyes of Nature? We all are born, we live, breathe, eat, defecate, reproduce, and die. Is that all? What about suffering? Is there any place in the plan for suffering? Does suffering have a purpose? Does suffering make us do things we would never have done had we not suffered? Does suffering create art and civilizations? Animals suffer too, but they never create anything for it. But they suffer, often silently.

That night, before we went to our rooms, I let Fabrice hold me. I did not resist. He kissed my cheek very tenderly, and caressed my lips with his fingers. He knew I was troubled, and he went no further. I slumped against him, and the warmth from his chest reassured me. Then he said goodnight. All thought of Graeth flew from my mind.

Misha invited us to tea the next day. Tea meant tea, although his wife was French. I noticed that the tea was served in the very Russian manner of filling and refilling the pot with hot water. The pot was a lovely faience in blue and green, short and stocky. The cups were squat with the same flowers. Misha's wife Nadine was in a very short dress, she was very pretty, and she had made apple tart. *Tarte aux pommes.* Very French. The boys, Mikhail and Leonardo, named after the two great artists, were very cordial and well mannered. The elder, about nine, bent low and put his lips to my hand. I found that charming and I said so. Nadine said, a little ruefully, "We have to pretend we are princes, so what if we are not." Perhaps the romantic lives of the Russian aristocrats in France had moved her.

"One day," said Tatiana, "like the children of many others who came away in the twenties and thirties, they will search for their Russian origins. But we are not from the aristocratic families ... that someone may have written our history; we are from the common stock. Just as those who came then and could not go back, and died longing for their country, in France or in America, we too can never truly be French, but then, is Russia the same? Where do we belong?"

Fabrice, however, was optimistic: "Migration is the destiny of human populations. From deepest Africa the human race emerged and diversified. Look where we are today. Perhaps erratically, in jerks and starts, but humans were meant to move, even in the present day, and ...not stay in one place forever. Think of the pioneers who went to America; they suffered too, but they did not go back to where they didn't have a living. To congested Europe. France is your home now Madame, it is a beautiful country. Look, look at the Alps: the Vercors, the Chartreuse, the Belledonne! They have welcomed you and your forbears."

Tatiana looked suddenly happier. She smiled and ate her apple tart, looking at the mountains that could be seen from where she sat, saying nothing.

I told Fabrice that we could leave Grenoble whenever he wanted, and so we booked our train tickets for the next morning. In the evening we strolled around the university area, and ate black and green olive pickles in vinegar, full green peppers and olive oil with bread, on a grassy bank by the highway, overgrown with ferns and dotted with daisies, in spite of the chill in the air, and I was contented. I wanted to return to my painting, to Dodi and Marina, to Monsieur Houllebecq's bookshelf, to Bernardo and Anita. To Paris.

We talked about this and that, nothing serious, and discussed cuisines of the North and South of France, as we ate the delicious baguette and pickles. We could see the Belledonne and the Chartreuse as we walked back, and my feet hurt from the cobbles on the roads. I was happy to be with Fabrice, and we held hands and walked because my feet hurt. Maybe we'd go to London together too, when Qadeer Mamoon, if Qadeer Mamoon got back from Pakistan. Yes, we would.

7
MARINA (THE SHADOW)

Marina Asturias was tending to Madame Desmoulins as she lay on her four-poster bed, hit by a crippling migraine. Her head was swathed in cloths heated and cooled alternately, dipped in rose-water and chamomile. The light fell on Marina's thick, dark hair growing very close on a low forehead, her eyebrows fine and winged, her cheeks smooth and ruddy, and her dark eyes bent in quiet compassion over her benefactress. Marina Asturias had a serene beauty that created around itself a mood, took for its own the objects around, the light and the movements of the shadows. The child was a plain and sickly one, outside the glowing halo of its mother, as if almost abandoned, despite her constant ministrations.

Each of us is like a teardrop fallen from the eye of Fate, rolling uncontrolled down the vestments of Destiny, partly absorbed, partly evaporated, before bouncing off into nothingness; some catch the light and shine bright a moment, some disappear in the darkest folds of the garment, and we are often helpless to even help each other.

When Madame Desmoulins at last fell into a doze, Marina and I went to the next room.

I had long been craving for the story of Marina, the Shadow, but to receive a story one must give one in return. So I told her about my life; I told her about *Isfahan,* our family house, beautiful and decadent, inhabited with shadows past and present; where I had grown up, where I had played with my cousins; and of Rahimganj, the small sleepy town where I had gone to school until I was sixteen.

I told her India is a complicated country.

That we lived in an area, where an ancient mosque had been taken apart brick by brick by extremists, under the eye of radical politicians, where a temple had to be built in its place, but more than a decade had passed, and the controversies could still not be resolved.

I told her of my shift to Nainital, of Rukhsaar, my room-mate, and of my all-consuming attachment to Rahul Ganguly, the young Bengali journalist. I told her of how Sister Augusta, my mother's friend, had been molested by fanatics in the church itself. I told her how my own mother had struck them both from behind the statue of a saint, with a workman's mallet. How a Christian boy had been arrested for the attempt to murder them. How Rahul, my first, and perhaps only love, had been threatened, then killed by extremists with a piece of the same stone the temple was to be constructed with, and of how my mother had gone away in a little boat, down the swollen river, never to return.

I knew she would understand me, believe me. Because only those who have tales of their own to tell believe the tales of others. So I also had the courage to tell her that in Grenoble, my mother's childhood friend had gone away down the Isère in a little boat, never to be seen again. I told her all this so naturally, while I had hesitated a hundred times before sharing it with Fabrice, who professed to love me.

When I spoke of my mother a sudden pang, a sudden emptiness, seemed to well in my insides; I had not wept for her. I had chosen to think she still lived, in me. I had not wept because my father had cried enough for us both. I had not wept because I thought I could still seek her out. I had not wept because there had been no shoulder to understand my pain, my loneliness, after her going. She had not been just a mother to me, but a guiding light, her simplicity and gentleness in spite of her intelligence was a rare and precious thing.

Suddenly I realized she was gone, gone forever.

I put my head in my hands and wept, haltingly, the sobs wrenched out of me, hurting my chest, my throat. Marina stood behind me, and put her arms about my shoulders. I felt a comfort I had not felt in days. Young as she must have been, there was a motherliness in her touch, a giving feeling, something warm, accepting, non-judgemental.

"You are lucky, *hermana*, that your mother loved you. So lucky." She called me sister. I, who never had a sister, not even a girl cousin to call my own.

Marina had had a mother, and many fathers. Men that could father children were not necessarily good men, she said. They were males but not men. Not fathers.

In bits and pieces, over the days, she reconstructed her life for me.

And I thought all the while, that in my own country, India, there were so many similar stories among the poor, but we took no interest in them, we left them to find their own endings.

"The Maya law does not allow one to steal children, but ah, *hermana*, that is what they do, that is what they do. When the Prince K'iche Achis tried to steal the Rabinaleb' children, he was put on trial, but when my Mekel was signed away, I knew nothing. I was ignorant and uncared for. Unlike your mother *hermana*, my mother was poor, illiterate; she had had no one to care for her either, so she did not know how to care for her children. And she had so many. But when my Mekel was born there was no one to give him the Three Breaths of Life that were to tell him who his ancestors were. The nurses did not let me see him, did not let me feed him. They thought he was up for adoption. I had signed him away without knowing. The lawyers who deal in these illegal adoptions send you to a place in San Pedro Epocapa, in Chimaltenango, where you have the baby."

"When I came to know, I fought to get my baby back. In Guatemala a mother can say no to a private adoption at any point in the process. The Solo Para Mujeres helped me. I stayed at a halfway home, run by a French organization, Les Trois Quarts du Monde."

"But when I met a man, Lorenzo, who promised to take me to America with him, the United States, I believed him. We travelled in a truck through Mexico. We had almost reached the USA, someone said; then at one point we were discovered; we escaped and we travelled miles towards the coast in a closed truck. I thought Mekel would die. Someone helped us get on an illegal boat to France.But when the boat started, Lorenzo was nowhere to be seen. I think he must have still wanted to go to New York. I knew he did not love me. Who can love anyone? My mother's lovers never truly loved her. She never loved her own children."

"I was afraid throughout the voyage. But I had nowhere to go. It took us many, many days. I cannot remember how many. Mekel was very unwell all through the journey. The deck hands ill-treated the refugees. We stopped at Port-au-Prince, for several days. A few runaways stayed on there. But something kept me on the ship. I stayed in a small cabin with a few other women. I rarely went out. There was little to eat. The ones who had some jewellery were better off because they sold it to the ship owners in exchange for food. Some prostituted themselves with the men on the ship. They brought food for me, too. I may have done the same, but Mekel was too little. The others helped me, or my Malko wouldn't be alive today."

"But when I reached France, I was not harassed by anyone. They helped me. I thought I had reached Paradise. Yes, for me this is Paradise. It is all Destiny. I have found a home and a mother. I have also found you, *hermana*. All my travails were not in vain."

"You might think I love Mekel because I loved his father, but no, Meyjumbee, I do not know who his father was. He could be anyone of the men who raped me. But I must love him because my own mother never loved us. My parents, they left us to be hurt by the world.A mother's love is needed to protect young ones."

Madame Desmoulins moaned in her sleep. "I will tell you more later," Marina looked lovingly at Mekel who was playing with some odds and ends on the carpet

I picked up my coat, embraced my newly-found sister, and left. Dodi wasn't at home, apparently. It was cold outside. I walked down alone to L'Esterel and ate a steak and fries. The waiter wasn't so friendly anymore. The American tourists for whom he performed were thinning out. The coffee I had afterwards tasted wonderful in the cold. I wanted to walk down to Pigalle, just for the fun of it, as there were lights all around, and music, but I was a little afraid. Since prostitution had been banned, any woman could be approached by a man; you couldn't identify a prostitute anymore.

An American friend of Graeth's had been accosted by a drunken man up the Rue des Martyrs once. He wouldn't believe she wasn't a prostitute. She had had to run, while he chased after her and abused her vilely. She managed to shut the glass door of her apartment building just as he caught up with her, and he kept banging on it and screaming, spitting on the glass, crying, "*Sale pute*!" She had been really afraid. Then she left the area and shifted to Montparnasse. I didn't dare venture out alone after dark once I'd heard her tale.

I did not want to call Fabrice. I saw his text message on my mobile. I did not respond.

The terrace of L'Esterel is on the street, but the street is sloping and the inner part of the café is below it. You can see the people walking above you in the street from the windows. I was sitting facing the windows, and I saw Dodi. For once he did not see me. He was with Manès Trigot. They were walking arm in arm, and Dodi leaned his head on Manès' shoulder for a brief moment. I was puzzled. He must really consider Manès his mentor and friend. The Snail and the Angel. Like the father perhaps, which Dodi never had. Manès Trigot didn't have a paternal personality, however, with his little hands spinning about on the axes of his wrists, his head with its light curls at odd angles on his neck, his pouty mouth betraying a childish weakness that is almost repulsive in a man, and often in a woman.

I saw them pass by, they walked slowly, like in a dream, Manès' pale eyes expressionless, looking skywards, and then I could see them no more. They were going up, towards the Rue des Norvins, I could tell. Dodi would go home. No math lesson today.

Fabrice was calling me again

The closeness that I had begun to develop with Fabrice could be taken no further because of my involvement with Dodi's family. A wall of my own constructing separated us–Fabrice belonged to a well-placed family, socially, economically–would he and his kind understand that people can live differently? That the joys and sorrows of the simple and afflicted are as important as those of the rich and comfortable? I felt intensely defensive of Dodi, Marina, Madame Desmoulins, the baby ... they were mine, for some reason, and Fabrice was the outsider, the scoffer, the insensible, the insensitive, the cruel rich, and I must hide from him at all costs the wounds, the suffering of my protégés. So my relationship with Fabrice suffered, and I did not even care to find out if he was all the terrible things I was accusing him of being, in my mind. No, I was too afraid to speak to him of all that was troubling me, all that was affecting me profoundly.

***

My heart is too small, my being too small," said Marina, sadly. "There is too much pain, too much death, too much cruelty in this world. I wonder if all the goodness can ever make up for it."

"*Por que? Por que? Por que*?" –Why? why? why? – rose from her throat in a strangled whisper. And I knew there never were any answers.

We sat in the *petit salon*, Dodi had again gone out on his bicycle, and Agnès Desmoulins had gone to Les Abbesses. "I had thought that if I have a girl, I will call her Rigoberta, after Rigoberta Menchu. But then Mekel came along, and I cannot even remember who suggested his name, but it is an old name, and if he did not receive the breaths of his ancestors, at least he could have an old name."

Was Marina Asturias' life intertwined with Agnès Desmoulins' as a trick of destiny, or was it because, for the evolution of the soul we must pass through a series of experiences that build a base of inner beliefs, for use perhaps … elsewhere?

I too, was there forever, in Marina's life, in Dodi's; a moment, and for always.

***

The geraniums on my window sill have bloomed. In the days turning darker, colder, it's strange. Strange also that the occasional bright sunshine patterns under the trees remain the same, the music in the metros plays on, only the music crosses the undefined line between the two worlds; the street musician remains on one side of the barrier, and the police cars wail insistently across the city.

When you wake, between the worlds of sleep and consciousness each truth seems possible, the impossible seems true, trembling like a dewdrop on a morning leaf, prepared to disappear with the first touch of the sun, dewdrops that witches gather; crystals that reflect the world and give answers.

Rainy morning. The apartment filled with grey light, creating images, lines, angles, corners, softness; a world inside, insulated from other worlds, a world beloved, because outside exists the kindness of strangers.

Monsieur Houllebecq has done me more favours than one – the bookshelves lining his apartment are filled with wonderful books, on art, literature, philosophy. I cannot read them all, nor understand the difficult French, but their very presence makes me feel I am in an exalted space. I can take them down and look at them. The illustrated volumes on art are those I can pore over, but even in the other books there are illustrations, and the faces of the philosophers look out from the pages, bringing worlds with them – Rousseau, Voltaire, Montesquieu, and the *Supper of the Philosophers*, an engraving by Huber.

There is a shelf with the beautiful volumes of Diane de Sellier's publishing, the *Fables* of La Fontaine with dozens of engravings as they originally were. I particularly like the *Self-Portrait of the Twentieth Century*, with Picasso, and Baudelaire's *Les Fleurs du Mal* illustrated with Decadent and Symbolist art… how much I have learnt from these strange and alien experiences, partly belonging to the Image World, available to all who care to take a peek.

I was wrong perhaps to reject the affection Fabrice was prepared to give me. Yet I thought, what is a life in which there is no connection with the afflicted? The other half? I had thought when I sat facing Fabrice at the Esterel. His face was so soft, so lacking in suffering. He had taken my hand over the table. His green French eyes glowed in the candlelight in his clear face. He was beautiful.

"Life, Fabrice," I had said slowly, "only takes on meaning when brought face to face with the life one *could* have *had*, or one could *still have*."

I thought he had looked sad. I thought he had my father's expression: sad because he could not understand. Could not understand why he had been cast outside the circle of the beloved. How could I tell him? The answers I was seeking lay not in the life he offered me. It would never make me a painter, because it would divest me of all true feeling.

I was fascinated not by his life, but by the lives of Agnès, of Dodi ... of Marina, by Agnès Desmoulins's window that looked out always, not at the vineyards of Montmartre, but at the blue of the Mediterranean.

I could almost see the sea myself, and all those lands far away that Agnès could see. I could see Emir's eyes, Monsieur Desmoulins' four curly-haired children in Skikda, and his second wife with a scarf around her head.

Only the occasional call of a solitary bird broke the silence.

That is when my painting *The Bereavement of Agnès Desmoulins* became a diptych. We know that every painting leads somewhere, into an emotional space that is not the physical space that surrounds us, that is part of the alternate world constantly spiralling about us, like the yellow fog of Eliot's *Prufrock,* revealing the little understood, but only in fragments. Just as the diptych forms the fragments of my painting. Realities are thus separated from each other and float around the world, confusing us, so that most of us choose to close our eyes to the larger picture, and find solace in the limited, the tangible, the enclosed.

We are so afraid of not being at all, that we are always in the process of becoming someone we may not be, and around the corner is Death; it comes to us in bits and pieces, we do not recognize it, for those bits are only bits of non-existence and death seems so much more dramatic. Like it had come to Emir.

And just as Agnès Desmoulins carried within her the Mediterranean she had never really known, in me the Isère too, had made a place, like the Gomti, in the throbbing of my pulse, in my breath, on my tongue, and in the manner the soles of my feet trammelled the earth as I walked on the hard, sloping Parisian pavements

***

Madame Desmoulins did not see me as she came out from her visit to Saint-Jean, and stood buying small grocery items at the Tunisian's shop next to it. I could hear her voice, but she was not speaking French, she was talking to the shopkeeper in fluent Arabic! She turned, she saw me and smiled absently. I said not a word, and we began to walk up together, taking, as if by mutual consent, the path towards the stairway.

"You speak Arabic?" I questioned tentatively.

"I did learn a bit from Emir," she said, in a non-communicative manner. "It does not matter."

I did not press her, but in a while she spoke again, lifting her head a bit, looking upwards in defiance, or in remembrance ...

"Arabic is a language inside me now; I don't need to speak it, I don't want people to know I speak it, because for me it has too many memories. It is part of me, just as Emir was, but the world does not acknowledge him in my life, nor ever did. And his language too, remains a part of me, inside, giving me comfort and inspiration–just as he did.That, Meyjumbee, is another me, not this French, Parisian me, but a 'me' that exists outside of all parameters and boundaries, a 'me' that has many more rhythms and cadences. A new language, an emotional addition, creates new rhythms that allow one to sail in different seas, on currents of air that flow in different waves, that pulsate to other, unknown beats; it is not just a form of communication with others, but with oneself. Can you understand?"

I did understand. Madame Desmoulins wanted to hide away that part of her, to now appear integrated, but the Mediterranean was inside her, as was the music of the Arabic tongue, and I could see it from her window. I could hear the songs of love, and the call from the white seaside mosques that were woven around her and would reappear in my painting, and the men and women Dodi could see, and I could.

"Did Emir have a beard?" I asked suddenly. Agnès smiled, a slow smile, full of meaning.

"No. He was clean shaven. He had a very refined face. He spoke very refined Arabic, unlike the *arabes du coin* who sell groceries. He'd been educated in Cairo and Paris."

We took the Rue Lepic past the Deux Moulins and began to discuss the film *Amélie Poulain*, because it had been filmed right there; the strangeness of the moment was put away for another rainy day: the sun had emerged for a short while, changing the way we perceived the world, as it is wont to do.

***

I met Graeth behind the basilica that afternoon; just where the hill fell away and you could see Paris, like a chalk-box in the mist. He wanted to do a portrait of me; I stood against the metal railing, and a bit of sun suddenly fell on my face, enough to inspire his portrait, he said, before the sky darkened once more. I pulled my jacket closer, shivering.

"You know," he began, "It was true what I said, the other day, that things are about to happen. There is a great unease in France. There are too many North Africans for this country to handle. They need them, yet they do not want them. You should go back to your country. There is a charge here … not good."

"That's what my father used to say about our little town," I remembered suddenly. Before everything happened. Those were Daddy's words too–*a charge*.

"I have to finish my painting, Graeth," I said, "You understand I couldn't do it back home now."

"Yes, yes, it's that Dodi, isn't it? Some things bind us to people and places, and we do not know why, but it does not happen to everyone, my little one, not to everyone. It seems a meaningless exercise sometimes. Yet Deleuze writes that sense or meaning, does not exist by itself, it is nothing but an effect, created perhaps through something that itself is without meaning; meaning need not be looked for and "found', but it must be produced, by creating signs, symbols, symbolic arrangements, devices, plans, that create meaning, and give a sense to everything. Have you read Patrice Maniglier? He says that meaning has nothing to do with an interior sense, but with the *way* sentences are used to manifest conditions that render them *true.* So Poetry, Art, Language all *create* meaning. And you need to do this in your own life at the moment. But my time in Paris is over now, I feel the need to leave it."

He walked up to me now and then, to turn my face this way or that, or to flick a strand of hair from my face with his pencil; I thought how much I liked him, his strange eyes, his long hands ... yet I knew that his absence would not make me suffer either.

But I must take his email address before he leaves. How else would I know what the Piper wanted to say? How would I be sure of my own ideas, my thoughts, my convictions without the support of the Piper? I thought all this as I watched him draw my features, his flaxen hair blowing about in the cold gusts, his angular face concentrated, but from the distance I could not see his pied eyes screwed up, the shadow of his crooked nose falling across his cheeks from time to time as his long lean fingers deftly manoeuvred paper and pencil over the board.

"Cynicism, Resignation and Faith are three sisters," said Graeth to me the day before he left, "You can choose to ride with any of them, the meaning is the same: that you have given up on the world or trying to change it. That you have given up on human beings."

"And which one have you chosen? " I asked.

"Certainly not Faith, not yet. A mix of Resignation and Cynicism, perhaps."

***

Then there were also two kinds of people; time and circumstance metamorphose or develop people in two different directions: the direction of those who can perceive things, and those that can not. For Marina, when she calls me *hermana*, it has more meanings than one; it means that I come from a country where stories like hers abound, and that they are accorded no importance because they are so plentiful.

Yet they are important, because they are all lives that could have been otherwise, better, more fruitful, happier; if the pursuit of happiness were allowed to human beings. I think some are just happier than others, and it's something that comes down from generation to generation, because of personal and social histories. Nothing, as was in my painting, is *today*, because it was something else yesterday and that yesterday cannot be effaced, and therefore the future too, is determined by what today is in the process of becoming depending on the reality that was *yesterday.*

Marina had been a very little girl when her parents separated and her mother did not have the means to feed her children, so she left them with their father. When you hear her story, you wonder if the Darwinism that my father always spoke to me about made sense in broken-down societies : he said the natural parent was always more inclined to look after its offspring, because it meant their genes were being carried forward into the next generation...that there were more abused children in broken families with step parents...but Marina's father had another woman who did not want Marina and her little brother, and, like the typical wicked stepmother, used to beat them cruelly until they had sores on their legs. The father watched all this without coming to their aid. When Marina's mother used to visit, the father and step mother would make the children wear full-length trousers and full-sleeved clothes to hide the welts and sores. Then one day, like in the story of Hansel and Gretel, at the behest of the evil stepmother, the father threw his children out of the house, and told them to go far away and never come back. Marina was five years old and her brother barely older; they spent the night on the roads, and wandered about, but luckily found their mother the next day.

Marina's mother soon took up with another man and had another baby; they lived together for a while, but like my father's Darwinism states, the new man started looking for fresh game, another female to impregnate, to forward his genes. He was unfaithful to Marina's mother and they broke up, and the natural father again left his child.

Apparently Madame Desmoulins was well aware of Marina's history, and it was she who completed the story that Marina had started, because Marina couldn't continue … it was too painful. Madame Desmoulins and I went for a walk and a coffee, down to the Opera, and all the way we talked about Marina and Madame Desmoulins' plans for her. From what I could see there was nothing concrete at the moment, except taking care of her and little Malko. Malko would go to the same school that Dodi attended, down the steps of the Rue Foyatier, and come back up as he used to, in the swinging shadows of the trees.

It was a stream of fathers that built a certain idea of a man in Marina's mind. Men use and abuse women, they impregnate them and abandon their children as well; that for a woman, pregnancy and childbirth are natural outcomes not of love, but of a certain kind of abuse, or prospect of abuse. And the only love that could exist was the love between a mother and her children, if it did, in fact, exist at all.

The worst part for Marina and her siblings was the time their mother became an alcoholic. When Marina's mother did not live in with a man, she used to prostitute herself to feed the children. Then one time she met up with a man who had a petty shop in the Mezquital, a shanty town. Many people who had run away from the highlands to escape guerrilla and military persecution had made their homes there. This new man used to drink away most of his money. The woman too began to drink, and she had child after child so that by the time Marina was eight, she had six siblings altogether. They used to have drunken quarrels, and the husband and wife beat each other up, beat up the children. They could hardly make ends meet. Marina's mother used to do odd jobs like grinding maize, or selling water at thirty centimes a barrel, making ten to fifteen rounds a day, to earn a little extra. When even this did not suffice she began to peddle drugs. Mezquital was full of drugs.

The stepfather's shop closed down because he never looked after it and was drunk on most days, and both of them became full-time drug peddlers. They didn't care if they were caught, they used to bring the marijuana leaves home when they were still green and dry them on the stove and on the roof of the hut when it was sunny.

But worse was to happen. The drunken stepfather, seeing Marina growing up, began trying to molest her, and hated her because she managed to get away each time. As often happens with children, adults don't believe them, because it does not suit them to. Marina knew this and never told her mother what was happening–she felt her mother would believe only her man. It was a constant struggle in Marina's life at that point, but she didn't feel so badly about it because the man was mostly weak with alcohol, and she could dodge him easily. The rest of the time she was out at school or babysitting.

As time went by, Marina's alcoholic mother became more and more degenerate until one day her best friend took her to the home of an evangelist. The evangelist promised her he would help her out of her alcoholism, and she converted herself to his faith. She sold her *Trajes* and *huipiles* for a few quetzals to an American friend of the evangelist; she started dressing like the Ladinos, in western dresses. Her man and she had a terrible quarrel over the idol of Maximon she kept in the house and now wanted to throw away. The evangelists wanted her to forget her old faith, and if they helped her, she would throw out Maximon, she said. Finally Maximon was put away in a cupboard in the daytime and came out only at night. It was a strange compromise the couple had made.

Marina's brother, Jose, because he was a boy, was allowed to stay out late and come and go as he pleased. He wasn't expected to do household work either. He soon joined a street gang, one of the *maras* operating in Mezquital, extorting money from local vendors, charging protection taxes, and also working in other poor areas in Guatemala City. Because he brought home money, his mother turned a blind eye to his activities. He used to tell Marina that he was proud to be a *marero* and that one day he would join the dreaded Mara 18. On the other hand, Marina, like many girls from poor households in India, had to fulfil different expectations. Half of the year her mother would draw her out of school because they didn't have the money, or she expected Marina, who was by now twelve, to work to help out with the family income.

School, for the little girl, was a place not to learn, but to meet her friends. She met Elivia, a bright and wilful child with red hair, whose mother, a Ladino (of Spanish descent), had died and whose father lived with a woman who didn't care about the stepchildren. Elivia loved the movies and often the two girls would bunk school to go to the cinema, which cost fifty centimes.

Once Marina's mother discovered her escapades, she began to punish her in various ways. She would send her to sell bread at the bus stand, and fetch fish from across the railway track. Often gangs of small boys like her brother's would snatch the bread and run away. Often she would be followed by young *mareros* who wanted to steal the fish she bought.

During these trips too, Marina would meet Elivia and they even made friends with some of the young *mareros*. Elivia had already got into sniffing gum, but Marina thought she would never drug herself.

The years went by. One day Marina's mother was really angry with her for being lazy, and it was late when she sent her off to the bus stand. Marina was alone. That was when the *mareros* followed her and raped her. They took her off into the bushes, tore off her clothes; four of them raped her, and she did not dare go home fearing her mother wouldn't believe her. So she went looking for Elivia who lived often on the streets, and Elivia took her back home.

Marina's mother was sorry, very sorry, for having sent her off so late at night, but all she did was take her to a doctor to see if she was pregnant and since she wasn't, the whole affair, the mother said, was best not spoken of ever.

Feeling more and more abandoned and betrayed, Marina left home, and her mother never went looking for her. Marina started to live on the streets with Elivia, and then began a life of drugs, thievery, alcoholism, which she hated. She had had an education of sorts, she felt what she was doing was wrong, but the street children were now her only family, and she had to do as they did. It so happened that by chance her mother saw her and sent her off to the reformatory prison for juveniles, with the help of the police. But Marina escaped from there a few months later and was back on the streets. She was drugged and raped by a group of drug dealers who had a lot of money, and that was when she became pregnant.

Elivia took her to a clinic where they said they would help her, but they had connections with illegal adoption agencies, and they persuaded her to sign papers for the adoption without explaining anything to her.

The rest, of course, she had told me already.

I thought the world a mad place; a cruel, mad place, I said, upon hearing her tale.

"No, *hermana*", she said sagely, "People are not mad, their spirits are inhabited by the *nahuales,* animal spirits, animal demons; my mother said the evangelists told her that."

I had read that the Ladinos and the invaders said *los nahuales* attacked their women and babies in the night, they were lycanthropes, werepeople, but the Aztecs believed they were each person's guardian spirits. Now it appeared even the spirits were at war with each other. One man's guardian was another's werewolf, naturally, for the babies of the invaders must fear; fear lest they be made to pay for what their forefathers had done to the indigenous peoples!

I woke up in the chill of the early morning, and the first thing that came to my mind, for a change, instead of the painting, was that I had twice seen Dodi with Manès Trigot. Surely Agnès Desmoulins was clinging to straws. Could Manès Trigot really be the mentor she was looking for, for Dodi? A man with so much racial prejudice? I had realized that after the incident in the metro. Could he really have sympathy for a half-wit, just because he was French? What about the fact that his godfathers had been Arabs? That should affect his judgment. Or, was it a taking back into the fold sort of thing for Trigot? I couldn't understand the man, and I did not like him.

I made some coffee, then went to look at the painting. It had a strange effect on me as always, as though it was a life I was being compelled to lead. I picked up my brushes and added a stroke to Dodi's arm, languidly lain over the sofa back. It looked even more languid, as if waiting. What was about to happen? In the painting? In the life of Agnès Desmoulins? I was certainly losing my mind. I felt I should call Daddy and tell him I was coming back soon.

But the painting held me in its grip.

What was I to do today? What was there to do at all? How long could I lead the lives of these people, in a country I was really unfamiliar with? Yes, to tell the truth, after the departure of Graeth, I felt suddenly orphaned. Fabrice was sweet, of course, but I think he failed to understand or perhaps appreciate the complexities of life in Paris. I accused him of too soft a life, too much security. He lived in the upper world, the white world, while Paris had long ceased to exist without its *émigrés*... Agnès' people, the people of my painting.

I dressed swiftly and thought I would have a quick apricot croissant at the piano bar and perhaps meet up with Bernardo and Anita. I'd learnt the man who stood at the take-away window of the piano bar was called Rézwan. He was Algerian. He was quite friendly when he had no customers. But when there was a queue outside the window, I saw a wild gleam in his eye, and he refused to recognize anyone he knew. I learnt that was his way, and I shouldn't take it personally. On the other hand the old French artist who stood with his easel, his back to the Sacré-Coeur, was a nasty piece of work if he thought you were only looking and not buying. The Americans had ruined everything, said Bernardo, from time to time. There was too much desperation for their dollars; the artists were like hungry rats scrambling after grain. The American tourists seemed to be running everything. He hated them, for their arrogance, he hated himself for needing their dollars. Americans were not the same as they used to be, when they had been indebted to Europe. Now, after the World War, Europe was indebted to them, and it would never change. Not in their lifetime at least.

I told Rézwan it was funny how welcome I was made to feel by the Arab community, although they themselves lived removed from mainstream life in many ways. Yet the French too were welcoming because I was Indian.

"The French love Youth," came the unexpected reply. "Not Indians or anything. Youth and Knowledge are the goddesses of the French, but they can never go hand in hand, so with Youth they must accept the beast of Ignorance, and with Knowledge they must show tolerance towards the Ogre of Old Age". I laughed. I tried to guess how old Rézwan might be. Not young, not old. Curly topped leathery face.

The Arabs lived in a world parallel to that of the French, that everyone knew. They shared a religion too. Even between them there were cultural differences and differences of dialect, but as the new generations began to forget Arabic, and they spoke only French, the distinctions began to get muted and slowly disappear. But the religion, Islam, still held them in thrall. It gave them their sense of belonging to a world larger than the one in which they were caught. Yes, in some way or the other each one felt trapped and isolated; the belief in a larger entity of which they too were a part, helped them look beyond their present circumstances.

Rézwan invited me to his home in Aubervilliers; he said his wife would cook some traditional dishes for me. They lived in a small flat, he told me, in a building where many other Algerians, Tunisians, Moroccans lived. It was old and dilapidated, but it was cheerful, with lots of children running about. One felt safe there with one's own kind around, he said.

The Tunisian girl at the laudromat, Aïsha, on the other hand, said she deeply appreciated the French. "They allow us to come here and work. We can earn for our children and our old parents," she said. "We should be grateful for the life we can have. Of course France will never be our own country. It cannot be. Some people think it is.

They suffer. They are angry. But me, the French have always treated me well. I love them. They are good, and kind and polite. It is up to us how we conduct ourselves. But then, you need to tell yourself, I am here to work, and I have a goal. I have not come here for love. Why should they love us? We are a different people. So different, so different. In my country, you hear the voices of people above all sounds. People yell, and they laugh, and they call out. Here, you hear the sounds of boots, of machines, of cars, of metros, of trains, of buses, but not voices, rarely voices."

"People travel and make new places their home. But it's not the same when your home is just across the Mediterranean. Your grandmother is there, your cousins who look like you, and the taste of the spices still on your tongue. One day you have to travel back. Then you can return if you want. But it is with the knowledge that there are two worlds. If you choose to live in this one you will have to learn the rules."

And then there was Agnès Desmoulins who had lived in another world by proxy; a world she believed she loved, and a language that had brought love to her.

***

It was early, but when I was leaving the building, I saw Manès Trigot enter, and we barely acknowledged each other. I don't know what made me turn back to look again once I had crossed the main doorway, and I saw him standing there, staring sadly at my back. Did he really believe, as Dodi said, that it was all my fault? Whatever that meant. My fault for doing what? I hurried away, feeling uncomfortable.

I was with Bernardo and Anita soon, and I forgot Manès Trigot. I told them Graeth had left, and that there was no news of him yet.

"Not a great artist," said Bernardo a little condescendingly.

"Even his portraits do not catch the right expression of the sitter." It pricked me somewhere to hear Graeth criticized. He'd gone, Graeth, but he had left with me the image of Three Sisters: Faith, Cynicism and Resignation, driving three fiery chariots.

"Sometimes an artist cannot translate his imagination onto canvas," I said defensively. "He had a great vision, Graeth."

"Then he should write poetry," Bernardo said dismissively. It was true Bernardo himself would have been a great painter. But he was too laid back. Anita said he did not work hard enough. He smoked too much.

"Ah, *cara*," responded the big man, twirling his moustache, "Life is meant to be lived, and not spent seeking recognition, and therefore suffering. When I paint, I am happy. Happier than when I'm doing anything else, except when making love to you."

That silenced Anita, I suppose, and she smiled a small secret smile and returned to her canvas.

"Van Gogh did not sell a single painting in his lifetime," Bernardo said, lighting his cigar.

Anita looked up, one eyebrow raised, "But he was doing something different, and that is really hard, doing something different from the norm. That is the hardest. And he stuck to it. He did not change because the world at that juncture did not accept his work. That is the test of fire."

"It is not only what you do, *cara*, it is how you do it. Michelangelo did commissioned work, but the emotion he put into it can still be experienced by the viewer. Ah, the *Slaves* in the Louvre, the Dead one, or the Sleeping Slave–how they make me weep each time I see them! They are more real than the living beings around them."

"When alive we are all pretending," countered Anita, "Our pretences are hung about us like cheap plastic flowers, hiding our real selves. If we were carved in stone, if there was an artist great enough to render us all as Michelangelo did the slaves, we would all be beautiful, and arouse emotion."

What emotion would a man like Manès Trigot arouse, if he were rendered in stone? I wanted to laugh out loud at the thought. Mirth, perhaps.

"Do you really believe, *cara*, that each one of us has that much emotion inside to provoke the interest of an artist?" Bernardo asked insightfully. "I know no artist would choose me for a subject!" he laughed then looked at me kindly. "Now here is a girl with a lost look in her eyes, a girl looking for her mother, a girl who knows inside that only in the seeking of Art can she find her; if I were a great artist, I would choose her, for inside her I can see the colours she is made up of, and the many expressions of her eyes and her face that need telling."

I was embarrassed, for although I had told them my story, suddenly to be reminded of why I was in Paris shook me up a bit. I felt as though he were glancing through me as through a transparent figure. And the truth was that only when I completed my painting would I feel I had in some measure vindicated the losses of my mother.

At that moment, luckily, I saw Marina come looking for me. She normally knew where I was in the mornings, if I wasn't in my room. And it was a pleasant day, less windy than most, and the sun had deigned to peep out for a bit. She appeared worried, and was alone. With whom had she left Malko?

"You must come with me, *hermana*", she said. "Dodi has packed a case and is throwing a tantrum. He wants to leave with Manès Trigot. She does not know what to do, poor Agnès!"

Bernardo had seen Marina for the first time. He was looking at her curiously.

"I could paint her", he said, "If I had the time. She is beautiful."

***

When I reached Agnès Desmoulins house with Marina, we found the door flung open wide. Manès Trigot stood with his arms crossed, a little away from the door, with a petulant expression on his face, his eyebrows raised in mild surprise, as if he were an innocent bystander. He was saying nothing. Dodi was quarrelling violently with his mother. She was almost in tears. Her face was flushed and her clothes dishevelled, showing she had tried for some time to bodily prevent her son from leaving. Dodi saw us then.

"Aah!" he cried flinging his arms above his head in a kind of despair, "*C'est elle*!" It is her! And with the Shadow! He threw down his case to which he had been clinging for dear life and rushed indoors, much to his mother's relief. She began to settle her hair and apologize.

"He said he would go away with Manès," she explained, "It's just one of his days you know."

Manès Trigot seemed to be edging away from our group; I walked up to him swiftly:

"Monsieur Trigot, you have nothing to say in the matter?"

Manès Trigot shrugged, looking innocent. "I can teach math, but this I cannot handle."

That sounded innocuous enough, and I let it go. But the incident in the metro had turned me forever against this apparently harmless and also helpful little man. I chided myself for being so judgmental, and turned to Agnès, who was still apologizing.

"Thank you for coming, Meyjumbee," she said, "I don't know what it is about you… this is the second time his tantrums have been cooled on your account."

Malko had woken in the inside of the house, and he called loudly for his mother. Marina hurried away indoors. Soon I was sipping tea with Madame Desmoulins and Manès Trigot in the *petit salon.*

"Dodi listens to you a lot, mostly. What would you have done if he had insisted on going with you today? Where would you have taken him?" I asked when Madame Desmoulins went into the kitchen for more tea.

I saw the little man smile for the first time, "*Vous blaguez, Mademoiselle!*" he said, you are joking, "I would've taken him for a little walk, and when he had calmed down a bit I would have brought him back. It's not as serious as it is made out to be. He has never run away before." Manès Trigot's pale blue eyes had a light silver sheen, I noticed.

In a while Dodi walked in as if nothing had happened. He motioned to me to follow him and went back into the gallery that led to the stairwell. It was a little dark in there, as the window pane was frosted and the day had turned cloudy. Already.

He stood there holding the banister. "Why do you think they came? Do you think they are still there?"

I looked steadily at him for a while. Then I decided I wasn't going to avoid this one now.

"You mean the people who were there when Emir died?" I asked

"Yes," he said, this time treating me with confidence and not like an intruder. "I know you saw them."

"It's okay, Dodi, I think they must have left. I put them in a painting, so I think they are not here anymore."

"You put them in a painting?"

"Yes, you can come to my rooms and see it if you like. If you put people in a painting, they don't come back anymore." That was a good idea, it seemed to convince Dodi. "But don't bring your teacher Manès Trigot."

"You don't like him, do you?"

"No, I don't mind him, but he is a stranger to me. I don't want him to see the people you and I see."

"He is the Angel. I am the Snail. Maybe if you put people in a painting or a sculpture they are just reborn elsewhere. Like me and Monsieur Manès."

We went back to the petit salon, and had tea and *pain au chocolat* that Marina had brought from the bakery. Manès Trigot left abruptly, with a small nod at everyone and a small noise issued from his throat that sounded a little like "*A bientôt*": see you soon.

***

That evening I was to meet one of my grandmother's publishers from Italy. There would be just me and him and perhaps Fabrice at the *Flore,* and I was happy because the *Flore* always reminded one that this was the place Sartre and Simone de Beauvoir used to spend many hours. Time goes by slowly in Paris. Dali's soft clocks are true for this city. Dancing clocks. Because here the Past confronts you tangibly at every corner. The Present, the Future, everything has to contend with the Past which is much stronger, with a vice like grip on the life of the city. In India we let our past die physically and live only in our memories. We worship the Goddess, create her image, love her, idolize her, then consecrate her to the waters to melt away until we choose to recreate her again. Everything is regenerated, renewed, reincarnated. The world lives in the minds of men there. Here, minds live in the world of stone and bronze, of icons and statues and inscriptions.

"You are the poet's granddaughter," said Signor Andretti.

I talked to him at length about the poems found in my mother's journal. No, they were not my grandmother's that was certain. I trembled inwardly, as I spoke to him, he was curious, of course. Luckily he was a busy man, and didn't pry more than was necessary. Time had gone by too, melted, like Dali's clocks. All considerations were commercial propositions as well. The few poems I had were not enough to excite even curiosity in a publisher. The poems of a dead woman. Why had my mother not wanted to even acknowledge her own work? She must have really had no confidence in her creativity.

Fabrice was looking very handsome across the table and once or twice his hand brushed mine. His skin was surprisingly smooth, and cool, like marble. He did not say much, and looked preoccupied with something.

Signor Andretti left in half an hour. Fabrice said he would drop me and then had a meeting. Of course I couldn't ask him what it was about, I had been ignoring him, all his advances, hadn't been sharing anything with him, what could I expect? We started walking out together in the evening chill, and the Flore glowed behind us. The bells at the Saint-Germain-des-Prés church were ringing. A ceremony? The wind blew the metallic bell notes hither and thither, so that they sounded sometimes low and sometimes louder.

At the metro station we said goodbye, because Fabrice had walked there from his office and he did not invite me to go back with him. He had a meeting with Jeannine, whoever that was.

"Do you feel happier now, *chérie*?" he asked abruptly.

"I think so, Fabrice. I shall go back soon. But I have some things to sort out before I leave."

"Anything you'd like to share with me?"

"You are so distant," I said, lowering my eyes.

"It is you who has kept me at that distance. Am I not right?"

"Perhaps you are. I am sorry. It is a hard time for me. I don't want to involve you in my crises."

"I've never said I didn't want to be. I was asked by my grandfather to take care of you."

"Did you want to?"

"You know I still do, if you'll allow me."

I found it hard to reply. What could I say? I did think that being a cry-baby on his shoulder might make him despise me. So I smiled, and so did he. My ego was intact yet. At least. Then he left. But I was softening towards him. He was a nice guy. He'd been very good in Grenoble.

I wasn't really surprised when he called me the very next day. Could we meet for dinner or lunch again? Or, just a stroll down to the Opera?

We ended up sitting on a park bench at the Buttes Chaumont in the nineteenth, under a thick bush. At first he held my hand in both of his and observed my nails. He wasn't smiling. I was nervous. Then he lifted it to his lips and kissed my fingers.

"Fabrice," I said, not knowing what else to say. Then he kissed me and I could feel the roughness of his jersey through mine. I felt warm and protected, and affection welled up inside me for this boy who had stopped teasing me and was kissing me with a fervour I hadn't expected. My loneliness melted away, his body against mine was like balm to my frayed soul, and I clung to him, never wanting to let go.

I realized for the first time since I had come to Paris, *I was there*. This wasn't happening to anyone else. It was an exhilarating feeling to suddenly *be there*.

"You know who Jeannine is? She is the girl I might marry. My parents would be happy. We are considered a couple already in publishers' circles."

"Then why me, Fabrice?" I asked, something squeezing my insides really hard.

"I don't feel about her the way I feel about you. You know there are certain things that cannot be explained in words?"

"But I ... I have to go ... back to India."

"You don't have to go."

"I must. Just as I had to come here, I know I must return, at least for now."

How could I ask him to wait and see how I felt after I returned home? It would be unfair of me.

It seemed as though he had read my thoughts: "You won't ask me to wait for you?"

"How can I? I can't promise anything. I am confused. I am too young to decide anything yet. I am homesick already."

"Do you plan to return home soon?" I couldn't make out if he was sad, though I wished somewhere that I could.

"I have some work to finish."

"Can I ask what that is?"

"It's a painting."

***

I lay awake that night thinking about Fabrice, the feel of his muscles against my shoulders, the roughness of his jersey, his hands on my cheeks; I longed for his touch. I knew he had broken the barrier that had built itself around me since Rahul had been killed, since my mother had died. What would happen to me now? I was no longer dulled to my own feelings.

It wasn't that late, it was just ten, I could watch some television. So I decided to get up, to calm my emotions, heat myself a cup of milk, perhaps, and as soon as I switched on the television, the doorbell buzzed. I went up to the front door hesitantly, for no one ever visited me, except Marina, who had come once or twice.

"Who is it?" I asked, a little afraid, "*Qui est-ce?*"

"Cest moi, Meyjumbee ! Moi, Dodi!," came Dodi's voice from the other side of the door.

I wondered if I should open the door at that time. Dodi wasn't always in his senses, what if he attacked me in some way? But I was curious, and quickly fetched my gown, to appear more presentable. Not that Dodi would've noticed.

Dodi shuffled in, haltingly, looking around as though embarrassed. I led him to the salon and switched on the lights. By this time I had guessed he wanted to see the painting.

"Where are they?" he asked softly, as though he would wake someone if he spoke louder.

I hesitated. He was in the picture too. Would he recognize himself? No, I supposed not. This was simply a game, or, was it? Wasn't there something strange about it all? Did those people in my painting exist for him as they did for me? Was I as crazy as this boy? What would he say? I was extremely curious myself, to know if we had visualized the same visitors at *The Bereavement of Agnès Desmoulins.*

I carefully removed the newspaper I had covered the painting with. Dodi was waiting eagerly, arms laid across his chest, like a connoisseur about to assess a work of art.

He was very still, very quiet, as the paper came crackling off the canvas. He stood there a good five minutes, staring. I didn't dare speak either, but I watched him and waited for his reaction. I saw his gaze scan the painting, then suddenly shift to the wall, and then around the room, as though there were other objects there that he had come to see!

He walked slowly out of the room, towards the door. He opened it with deliberate movements, and it was only when he reached the landing that he spoke.

"There were more of them. But you did not see them. They may be here still."

"How many more?"

But he did not reply and went down without saying goodnight.

I shut the door and went back to the painting. The Pied Piper's eyes appeared like those of the famed paintings of the Mysore Palace, following you wherever you went in the room, and I didn't know how to use that technique at all …

What about the others that Dodi had seen? That I had not? Where were they? And would he speak about my painting to Manès Trigot? Surely he would. It was a very uncomfortable feeling, thinking that Manès Trigot would know about my work. Even knowing was a sort of communication; I didn't want to communicate with the little Frenchman at any level. Now there was no help for it, so I returned to bed, and luckily by this time I had forgotten about being in Fabrice's arms, so I went off to sleep almost immediately.

***

Isabelle arrived that weekend with her haughty offspring, and a small gentleman in a grey suit and round glasses, a very soft spoken and self-effacing man, who went up to Dodi's room with Dodi while the rich brats played and chattered in the *grand salon*, which had been specially prepared for the morning. I was there by chance as I'd gone to return a book I had borrowed and was invited in by Madame Desmoulins, to keep Marina company. Manès Trigot was there too, and I noticed that when Isabelle was around his manner became obsequious and a simper adorned his pale countenance throughout—he was obviously impressed by her affluence and style, as well as her social status. He hung around making insignificant little remarks and shrugging his shoulders at appropriate junctures of the conversation, which centred around Dodi, and he was included, as he was his tutor.

I helped Marina make coffee and set out the *viennoiserie* in trays and felt very much a part of the family, except for Isabelle's brats for I couldn't understand a word they said, so full of argot was their language, so full of expressions one normally didn't hear in the street. Isabelle had brought Mekel a gift of a beautiful cloth book for children and he was busy flipping the pages on the carpet, not looking out for his mother for a change.

In a while the counsellor, Monsieur Morin, and Dodi, came down. Dodi and his cousins were sent off to the smaller salon.

"He has a few issues," said the counsellor. "He wants be able to go out more often with his tutor, and he promises to return home by the evening. Also, he no longer wants to be called Dodi, he wants to be addressed as Jean-François all the time."

Madame Desmoulins looked a little crestfallen I could see, but Isabelle responded matter of factly, and her sister's expression eased. "*C'est normal,*" she said, "Of course we'll comply with his requests,that's not a problem, but he mustn't try and run off on his own."

"I think if he is allowed to go out with this Monsieur Trigot, in whom he seems to have a lot of faith," said Monsieur Morin, "he may not want to run away suddenly. Some feelings of suffocation are normal in his condition, you will agree. Now we have to know whether Monsieur Trigot is willing to take on this responsibility." The doctor turned towards Manès Trigot.

"*Bien sur*!" Manès Trigot shrugged magnanimously, and his little hands, resting on his knees, swivelled once on their axes, like a *Kathak* dancer's.

So it was decided that on some weekends Manès Trigot would take Dodi out to the museum, to the park, to the Géode, perhaps, to the Parc Zoologique.

I wasn't satisfied, but I had to keep my opinion to myself, since no one was asking me. But I had heard that it was only of late that Dodi had wanted to make such excursions, it hadn't been a routine behaviour with him since childhood, and I felt Manès Trigot must have had a hand in it.

***

It was perhaps fortuitous, meeting Manès Trigot at every street corner, and I discovered him one day emerging from a seedy looking store at the corner of Rue des Trois Frères. My French and my confidence had been getting better and better as the days passed and I let go of my uncomfortable diffidence and allowed my curiosity about the city full rein. I entered every shop, asked questions, and ignored those who were cold with a smile.

Just outside this shop was a pavement bookstall and I stooped to browse the books sold for one euro or two. From within emerged Monsieur Trigot, accompanied by a golden-haired middle-aged woman wearing rather a quantity of coloured baubles and a flowery cotton kurta, her eyes heavily kohled. He addressed her as Dominique, as he bid her goodbye. Luckily he was going in the other direction and did not spot me, but the moment I rose from my stooping position Dominique smiled at me and addressed me in Hindi, "*Kya haal hai?*" she asked. How are you?

She took me into her shop and said she organized "spiritual tours" for French and even American citizens; tours to India. I looked around the little space: there were pictures of Hindu gods and goddesses from cheap calendars pasted on the walls on one side, on another were temples, including that of Angkor Vat, and on one wall were the tour packages advertised. Meditation, relationships, alternative healing, ayurvedic massage …

A small chat with her revealed that she did not know the difference between, or even the names of, the Hindu gods. I wondered what Manès Trigot had been doing in that shop. Surely he wasn't the kind to entertain exotic thoughts. If anything he seemed the kind of person who would never socialize with any different race or creed.

I decided I was wasting my time, and these agencies were interested in conning lost souls into paying heavy prices for "spiritual" packages. We had enough in India and there was nothing that could be done about them. She must have realized I wasn't her type either, for she did not press me to stay longer. As I was bidding Dominique goodbye, a young Indian man in a green army jacket strolled up and stood at the door. Dominique handed him a small paper packet and he gave her some money. He hardly spoke the language, and communicated more with nods and waves of the hand, and his large watery eyes.

I followed him to the Square Charles Dullin, where he parked himself on a bench, rolled a narrow cigarette, and began to smoke in a melancholy kind of way. I sat at the terrace of the café opposite and ordered a coffee. I saw behind the bench a shorter, younger, Indian man, asleep in a tattered sleeping bag. The tall one woke him presently, prodding him time and again, and they proceeded to have some kind of argument, following which the smaller one got up, crossed the road from across my café and merrily peed on the wall of the building opposite, which was under repair. So that's what all those marks on the wall were, I thought. The smaller man then went towards the Tunisian store and disappeared into it. I saw the tall one looked sadder and sadder on his bench under the trees. Driven by curiosity about a fellow countryman I casually walked up to him, and spoke in Hindi. He answered in Punjabi, which I understood for the most part.

"Are you unwell?" I asked. His cigarette had a peculiar sweet smell and although I had no experience of it, I thought it must be hashish. That's why he looked sad and his eyes watery, I thought. But the moment I enquired if he were unwell he broke into loud sobs. I was perplexed. He explained, wiping his eyes like a child with the back of his large hands, that he was from the interiors of Punjab, his uncle had promised him and his brother jobs in Canada, brought them to Paris where he took their passports and disappeared, leaving them stranded. He said he was a Sikh, but had cut off his hair and shaved his beard in order not to be noticed in a crowd; he missed his mother and sisters, he wanted to go back but now he never would until he had made something of himself. Why didn't they go to the refugee office, I asked? He said they would deport them to India as they had no papers, and that he would rather die than go home without making something of himself. At that moment the shorter one came jogging up, and the taller one, who told me his name was Sukhi, stopped crying. I was about to leave when the wail of police sirens filled the square and people came out on their balconies and out of their shops to look. Two police men strode towards the Punjabi boys and whisked them into their car. The cars went away, wailing loudly.

I asked a shopkeeper where they would take them. He smiled and said, ah, nowhere, they would yell at them and let them off at the end of the next road. That happened from time to time. This was Paris, he said, a lot of folk lived here illegally, the police also knew that, and didn't want to take too much trouble. The illegal people disappeared after a time, found their way out to other countries or their status was legalized, or they went back home. He told me Sukhi and his brother had been sleeping on the pavement there for nearly four months. Poor Indian boys, I thought.

Sure enough, I saw Sukhi the very next afternoon, selling tickets for the toy train that takes tourists around Montmartre. He looked through me, and I too decided not to acknowledge him. In my own country, anyway, I would never have gone up to a strange man to chat. It was too dangerous for girls to do that.

***

It was Fabrice's birthday the next weekend and I went with him to his parents', who lived sometimes at Vésinet-le-Pêque, in a little cottage surrounded by a lovely landscaped garden and tall sycamore trees. The party was a daytime affair, under the trees even in that windy weather, because the sun did show up now and then, suddenly lighting up the scene with a surprising brilliance. The garden had beautifully designed furniture all in rough seasoned wood of a greenish-brown, and the cakes and tarts were all home made, Fabrice's mother said. She was a smart woman in a dark sophisticated dress, and her husband, whom I had met before, was a large Frenchman, rather like Gerard Depardieu. Jeannine was there, a petite brunette with a perfect face, and Fabrice's parents made much of her. They were nice to me, but obviously they were close to Jeannine. However, there were many guests, and it was a hilarious, friendly affair, everyone in high spirits, especially after a few bottles of wine had been downed. I didn't have to do much talking; I sat with a glass of Chardonnay and looked on, and listened, taking in the scene truly like an outsider. Fabrice did not pay me any extra attention for which I was grateful, as Jeannine was there, and with the little I had to offer Fabrice, I thought it better if he spent time with her rather than with me.

No, I did not belong here. Even if I were to marry Fabrice, could I stay on here in this world and adjust without compromise? It was a lovely life, but it wasn't mine. I did not aspire for it either. It began to rain and each person picked up something and ran laughing into the glass room in the front of the cottage

It continued to rain and Fabrice decided to drop me all the way back to Montmartre, as it was late. When we arrived at the building, Fabrice said he would come up and if I could offer him a cup of Indian tea. I was imagining, hoping for, I think, another romantic interlude with him, a few more stolen kisses. But we found Dodi standing in the quadrangle in the rain, looking dolefully at my window facing the courtyard.

He brightened when he saw me. "Can I please see them again?" he said in pleading tone.

"No, Jean-François," I found myself saying "I have a guest. I am going to make him some tea."

"I will have tea with you, too", said Dodi, quite firmly "and do you have any chocolate croissants?"

"Who's he?" Fabrice wanted to know. He looked quite foxed. I motioned to him that I'd explain later. But Dodi did come up with us, even though I said I could substitute the chocolate croissants only with butter biscuits. I knew Fabrice was disappointed and so was I, but that couldn't be helped now.

I introduced Dodi as Jean-François and told him I wouldn't let him see the painting today.

While I was making the tea in the small kitchen, I could hear Dodi tell Fabrice that when he was allowed to vote he would vote for the Front National. He said Monsieur Trigot always voted for the FN, and that was best, because when they came into power only the French would live in France and all the immigrants would have to go. The French National character would be preserved. Fabrice called out to me: "Very right-wing, your young fellow here!" I gestured to Fabrice when Dodi was looking the other way that he didn't know what he was talking about.

It was a stilted tea, with Dodi and Fabrice, and all three of us drank tea and ate butter cookies without a word, after which Fabrice said he had to leave. I saw him to the door and Dodi followed me, standing behind me, so I couldn't even kiss Fabrice goodbye.

Fabrice smiled amusedly, and said "*Tant pis*!"— Too bad. I saw the funny side of the situation and smiled and waved goodbye from the small balcony outside the French window as he left, and Dodi stood behind me all the time.

Fabrice asked me over the phone the next day what the painting was all about, who Jean-François was, and why did he want to see the painting. I really did not know what to say. His love for logic was so great, how could I tell him what I believed, what I felt? I knew even then that one cannot base one's life upon intuitions and beliefs that have not been corroborated by reality, but for a poet or an artist the need to verify creative impulses could be very tiresome. Of course I had not seen the people in my painting. Of course a double existence is only in the mind, of course … many things. Yet.

"Oh, Jean-François thinks he saw the people in my painting in his home. He's a little off centre you know. One has to humour him. He's my neighbour's son."

"Ah," said Fabrice, "*Un illuminé*!"(An illumined one, as they say in France!)

"The people in my painting … what inspired me? Well, when you see it perhaps I will tell you … yes, yes, it's figurative."

He was very chatty that morning. He said there were many right-wing people in Paris. Jean-François seemed to belong to such a family. I assured him Madame Desmoulins wasn't one of them.

"The thing to do," he said, (one of their authors has been commissioned to write a book on this topic) "… is to help develop the countries that France colonized, the Congo, Senegal, Tunisia, Benin, for example. Then there will be less influx into France if jobs and educational opportunities were created in their own country."

"You also believe in conserving the pure culture of France?" I asked

"Not in the sense you mean, my dear. I believe in balance. Unlike in America, which is geographically much larger, where the Amish can exist, and all social groups, the Jews the Muslims, are encouraged to retain their separate cultures, in France we are "*laïque*" in the true sense. We are not for *communauterisme*."

In India, on the other hand he said, we encouraged *communauterism*, I agreed and said we were allowing a minority of bigots to set the rules for a larger majority, but the larger majority seems to comply, and religious beliefs or superstitions founded court decisions at times. I said we gave too much importance to religious heads and now we were reaching a stage when even a *lack of belief* was seen as disrespect, and the religious heads were mostly men, and they made all the rules for women, that was the strangest part.

But again, why did India always turn up in the conversation as a means to justify the racism in France?

"Its not as simple as that," Fabrice said, "its not only racism that is the problem, and what you see today of France, the unemployment in the ethnic minorities, which can go as high as forty percent in the suburban areas where they live in the housing created for them by the government..."

"What is it, then? Why don't they get white collar jobs, even if, I have heard, they have the same qualifications as the white man?"

"I am not denying there is racism," Fabrice said, "but globalization is playing a very important part in the problems of the immigrants. You see they came here and they had jobs, in factories, in establishments that needed them at the time. Today because of globalization these factories have closed down. The jobs that were being done by, say the Tunisians in France, are now being done by Tunisians in Tunisia—you understand?"

This time to make an analogy with India seemed appropriate, because the same had happened there, I had studied that in economics at school and then at college. Unemployment had increased because of globalization. There was no job security any longer. The men, who were skilled labour and had to be paid a certain minimum amount set by the government, had been laid off. The women were employed as home-based workers or as unskilled workers doing the same jobs but not able to draw the same salaries. No labour laws were in place for home-based workers in India. Middlemen exploited them to the hilt.

But in India, I thought, people were fatalistic. They were used to a classist ideology, and they were Indians, whatever class, race or religion they may be, they had nowhere to go; nobody spoke to them of "*liberté, fraternité, egalité.*" Although the Constitution said we were all equal and had equal rights, centuries of subjugation, and class differences had left the underprivileged Indians almost apathetic to their own condition. They were believers, they prayed to the Almighty to solve their problems. The State would offer nothing to the destitute individual. Distress, discontent, alienation, then, would emerge in different forms, as religious conflicts, as Naxalite movements, as Maoist movements, as linguistic or regional conflicts. No one seemed to be actually fighting for their right to a dignified life. The theory was all in place, but it did not reach the people in practice, no not even to their minds; the theory itself wasn't known to them. All movements turned into Frankenstein monsters devouring everything around them. I said this to Fabrice, and he replied that he believed even religions were Frankenstein's monsters.

The more we discussed these subjects the more respect I developed for Fabrice, the more I evolved and was drawn to reasoning things out for myself, to seeing connections, but the less I could talk about Dodi to him, about Marina and Mekel, about Madame Desmoulins.

The following Wednesday I saw Manès Trigot and Dodi through my window that overlooked the courtyard. Dodi had a duffel bag on his shoulder, a small one, not the case he had been running away with. Manès Trigot walked quickly, taking stiff little steps, his pointed shoes shining in the morning light. Dodi looked pale and faded in a deep blue polo-necked pullover, and his hands shone white and big as he swung the bag over his shoulder. But he had a smile on his face. I wondered where they were off to. I couldn't follow them, of course, that would be too obvious. And what if I discovered something untoward, unpleasant, about Manès Trigot, would Madame Desmoulins have the courage to send him off? Like what had he been doing in Dominique's shop, for example? Was that enough to disqualify him as mentor for a half-wit? Who would care to mentor a half-wit called Dodi anyway?

I phoned Marina and asked her if she would like a walk around Montmartre sometime later. She said Madame Desmoulins wanted me to come over, as Dodi had left with Manès Trigot for the day. I was only too glad to be invited early in the morning, and I asked if I should bring my breakfast over. Marina said that was okay, and I picked up my baguette and rolls and as soon as I was dressed, I tripped over happily across the quadrangle. I looked forward to getting to know more about Marina, and more about Madame Desmoulins.

They were watching TV, the news, when Marina let me in. Malko was on the rug, eating porridge from a large plastic bowl on which a picture of Obelix was printed. It was cosy inside, although the wind blew in sudden gusts outside. It tossed about the few leaves which it had shaken off the trees. It blew away the mist from the Allée des Brouillards, I imagined, and I felt sad thinking about Nerval.

The door of the *grand salon* was open and sunshine was slowly creeping in as the sun rose higher. I sat on the sofa in the *petit salon* and dipped my *petit pain* in a large mug of the coffee Marina had made. Madame Desmoulins came in from the other room, which she had been settling.

"See the things in my house?" she asked. "Look at the drapes, the curios, the paintings, the furniture; there are too many things I can call mine. But what do I have really? What can I truly call mine?" A life by the Mediterranean, a life of white walls and blue sea and nothing else. A life without Dodi?

Agnès walked to the mantelpiece over the hearth, dusted it quickly and laid her head against the cold green marble. She seemed like someone trying to soothe a headache. She lifted her head and smiled at me, a simple smile.

"Once I have settled Dodi, I shall book myself on tours to see Europe, and perhaps the world. I need to travel. The same scenes day after day fatigue me."

"Cant you leave Dodi for a weekend and go somewhere?"

"Ah no, Meyjumbee, no. He can be uncontrollable. Isabelle can take care of him, perhaps, but her children … you know, they might tease or taunt him. I could go, if Dodi were married." she appeared lost, quite suddenly. "If someone loved him as I do."

"Won't Manès Trigot help?"

"How could he? I can't ask him to come and stay here. No, Meyjumbee, until the time comes for me, I cannot go. One day that time will come too."

Marina looked sad. If Madame Desmoulins left, she would again be alone. She helped Mekel with the last bits of his porridge, scooping the remains up with the spoon and shovelling them into his mouth quickly.

"I have travelled, travelled far to be with you Agnès," she said, "This is my Paradise."

"And I have to seek mine," responded the lady with equal conviction. "If only there was someone to take care of Dodi during my absence. You cannot, not yet. Maybe one day you will be able to."

"Yes," said Marina, "When Malko is older, I will be free to."

Malko will become older, start school, I thought, that was a future one could depend on, at least… but Dodi being married? What could Agnès Desmoulins be thinking of? Who would marry an *aliéné,* a *jobard*, a simpleton? Someone who needed to be looked after forever? I knew parents were often in denial about the problems and the future of their special children, but this was extreme—Dodi, married! I felt a pang for his mother strike at my heart. Poor Agnès! Would her dream of discovering new lands remain as unfulfilled as her dream for her son?

8
Lunch at Aubervilliers

Rezwan came to pick me up and as I set out with him, I saw Dodi looking out from the window, with a scowl on his face. I waved to him, but he didn't wave back.

Being on the metro in the late morning with Rezwan, whizzing away towards Aubervilliers, where he lived and Abdurraheim lived, meant I was taking risks my upbringing wouldn't approve of—but what the hell! Nobody knew I had to make that jump in Time, because my mother had been sent backwards in Time by my grandmother, my *Nani*; married off into a small town, trapped in a mediocre life when her mother herself had lived independent and free. *Nani* had trapped my mother, and my father had trapped my mother like Monsieur Séguin's goats, when they needed to eat the fresh mountain grass, when the wolf would be waiting for them, but all night they would battle him, and death would be sweet … sweet as the fresh mountain grasses, for the taste of which one could risk anything … anything at all. I had to cross over bridges left uncrossed, live that life left unlived, discover that heritage which was due to me … only, I did not know the way. I did not know the way.

Across and upon the canals of the Seine, Aubervilliers is an industrial township, and Rezwan's brother lives in the flat next door, he told me on the train. He works in a leather factory, not far from their HLM. I had never seen an HLM before, *Habitation à Loyer Modéré*, lower income group housing. We walked from the desolate, graffitied, dingy metro station towards the market and then to a conglomeration of yellowish flats, of five to seven stories. If I did have an idea of the poor living conditions of immigrants in Paris, I was still taken aback at the utterly utilitarian aspect of the area, its unkempt parks, its undecorated streets, the school within stone walls, from within which the resounding calls of hordes of children issued like a prophetic echoing. The half-torn posters on the otherwise bare walls of the shopping complexes were as desolate as the metro station had been. The wind blew about bits of paper around the tired feet of podgy women wheeling shopping carts. This too was Paris. I felt depressed.

Rezwan was talking cheerily all the time, however, and did not notice my mood. He was telling me about his children Qadir and Ahmed Messali, (both named after Algerian revolutionaries), and the dishes his wife Ferhat would prepare for me and how they would compare with the spicy dishes of India.

We walked across a small parking lot into one of the yellow buildings. The entrance was not large, and there were several bicycles stuffed under the stairway. The lift had to be kicked to life. It was full of graffiti but Rezwan was still talking on contentedly, telling me how well his children were learning at school.

The apartment was small but with large windows in the living area. They looked out into the branches of a tree, which cast a pleasant green light into the room. As I entered, the flavour of good cooking enveloped us, and there was an immediate warmth that emanated from the house. Music was playing in one of the rooms; there was a bright carpet on the floor upon which a large woman in traditional robes sat peeling a variety of fruit. She stood up as we entered, and smiled. She had large dark eyes, and curly hair. She would've have been about thirty, but walked heavily, like a much older woman.

No, that wasn't Ferhat, his wife, Rezwan said, that was Khadija, his *sister in law*. Ferhat emerged from the kitchen and enveloped me in a large hug. She too was a smiling woman, and I noticed that she wore no scarf either. She said she was happy to see me, a sister from the other side of the world. I was her sister too, just as I was Marina's. And at that moment I felt it was true. There was a sisterhood that was far deeper than brotherhood, which spanned continents, and races, and seas, and countries and classes. Only those women who identified with and upheld the hierarchies and divisions created by men could not experience that sisterhood, and I was suddenly sorry for them. Those were the women who were not free. Scarves and *burqas* and all that men could impose upon women were but symbols of an exterior subjugation, but left spirits intact, unbound, unless women themselves chose to be subjugated by believing what the men believed. Short skirts, and low necklines, and wine and cigarettes and easy sex and even high corporate positions were no indication of real freedom. Real freedom was the ability to think beyond the parameters set by men, the freedom to love, and accept. Often the most subjugated women are truly free and the apparently free women are slaves to the system.

I had taken a box of chocolates for the children, but gave them to Ferhat as the boys weren't around.

I noticed that the door was left open and we could hear people passing by in the corridor. A very young woman in trousers and a head scarf came rushing in, holding two toddlers by the hand. She wished everyone quickly, said something to Ferhat in a mixture of Arabic and French, and rushed out pulling the children behind her.

A few minutes later another young woman, tall, black, came in to greet everyone and left in the same way. Obviously they knew all the inhabitants of the building, and were popular.

Just as Rezwan had been, Ferhat too, was keen that the meal she had prepared be very enjoyable, and a time of sharing and discovering likenesses; we were to eat before the children came home from school. We sat cross legged on the carpet, and a low folding table was set before us, a clean cloth spread over it, and the dishes brought out. There was the *chorba*, or soup—which in our area of Uttar Pradesh we call *shorba* in Urdu, and pronounce it almost in the same way, meaning the curry—Ferhat explained to me that there were two kinds of *chorba*, the *Beyda* or white and the *Hamra* or red. We had *chorba beyda* that day. Then there was *reshta,* with semolina and *tagliatelles* and lamb, a kind of spicy rice *pulao* with chicken, and *tagines El Khoukh*, which were shaped like peaches but were actually meatballs. How nice of them to invite me, how generous, I thought gratefully as I relished the food. How awfully friendly! To finish, there were *dziriyetes*, kind of yellow almond cakes, which they had bought from a store, as they were not so easy to make perfectly, Ferhat admitted. And of course Khadija's fruit.

Khadija, ate with us, but her husband was out working in the leather factory. Her brother had been killed in the Kabylie upsurge. She was from the Kabylie region of Algeria, and her brother had been part of the movement in 2001 against the Arabization of the eighties. I was surprised to learn that many Algerians were Berbers, and that Arabic wasn't their mother tongue. I blushed inwardly at my ignorance. They were the Imazighen, or, that she was an Amazigh woman.

"Ah, what Algeria was during the Ottoman Empire, what it has now become," lamented Rezwan as he ate. "We used to *own* the Mediterranean! The Europeans couldn't cross without paying taxes! Otherwise we would capture and ransom their ships. For three hundred years! Can you imagine that power? But the French, they turned us into servants, peasants, and no non-white after 1834 was allowed to hold a good post. They crushed us. Now we are nothing but a nation warring with itself, and for the occident, all wars which they support serve a purpose— to keep other countries destabilized"

"Do you want to go back, someday?" I asked

"To what? Here we earn a living. Our children are getting an education. They can never go back. They belong here."

"Do you wear scarves in your country?" Ferhat asked me.

"There is no compulsion," I responded "It depends on the family, the region. Although if the religious heads could have their way they would put all women in veils, but they don't have the power. We are a democratic country, a secular one. And Muslims are a minority."

"How nice!" Ferhat said, "I myself am a follower of Dounia Bouzar, who is half- French, half-Algerian. She believes, as I do too, that political leaders cannot and should not define what we are as French Muslims. It's up to us to say who we are, who we want to be. She does not wear a scarf herself, but thinks the French government has no right to ban it in schools. Freedom should work both ways."

True, I thought. Girls should be allowed to wear scarves if they couldn't get used to the idea of taking them off, if it distressed them. I couldn't imagine an Indian girl going without her *dupatta* when in a *shalwar* suit, although otherwise she may wear jeans and tight T-shirts.

Suddenly there was a commotion on the stairs, and two tall boys burst into the room. They were shy and loutish at the same time, as adolescents tend to be, and smiled abruptly, then averted their faces, then said something to each other that no one else could follow, and in another noisy burst of energy they were out of the room. Ferhat looked after them indulgently, and said they were to immediately wash their hands and faces and present themselves at the meal.

Rezwan said once more that they were doing well at school, but he was sorry that they spoke little Arabic and almost no Tamazight, the language of the Imazighen. They were most comfortable in French. They disliked going to the mosque too, although they agreed to say the *namaaz* occasionally at home.

I saw that Khadija had moved to the window and was looking out at the tree with a strange expression. She too must live in many worlds, I thought. All their spirits seemed to be swaying like pendulums between two worlds. The world they couldn't inhabit, but which inhabited them. And the world they lived in, but which did not touch them deeply enough to call their own. Tatiana too had been fragmented in spirit, but she had integrated with the French in the next generation; for the Muslims, however, the integration would be only at an abstract level, with a larger Islamic world, which was not a white world.

If I married Fabrice and stayed on in Paris, I too may live in two worlds, one at the level of the spirit, and one at the level of the physical being. Then I would live in three worlds, for the image world, the interior world of Nerval, of Dali, too, claimed my interest. It was, at this moment, selecting and cutting out Khadija by the window with the tree, ready to paste it onto another reality.

***

I returned alone, and it was getting dark. As I entered the courtyard I spied Dodi pacing up and down, scowling. He immediately walked up to me.

"Where have you been?" he asked, proprietorially. "*Aubervillie rs*," I replied smiling, for I was getting used to his ways.

"Did you see them all?"

"No," I said, lobbing this one off skilfully.

"But you went with him … he must know them."

"No, Dodi," I calmed him. "There was no one there." But I knew he was right, they were there. Khadija had been there, more than anyone else. Yes, she was there.

"All right," he said, "Then give me the address of the place you went to!"

"Okay, I promise I will," I said, still trying to placate him. "Tomorrow."

He went away without a word after that. I hoped he would forget by the morning. But I knew I had to put Khadija into my painting. Yes, she had been there.

***

Somehow Dodi the Beloved, followed me to Place du Tertre on Wednesday, and insisted I ask Rezwan his address. I humoured him, and we went to Rezwan's outlet window. There were a few customers he attended to, after which he greeted me cheerfully, as always, and he was a little surprised, but told me his exact address. I wrote it down on a scrap of paper and gave it to Dodi. He looked happy and went off. It was Wednesday and his tutor Manès Trigot would be there in the afternoon to teach him math. I saw him skipping away down the road, in his heavy, lumbering manner. Rezwan and I exchanged a few pleasantries, and cursed the weather, which was getting gloomier by the day.

I went to the internet café by the metro Abbesses, run by the Pakistani family, to check my email. No, there was nothing from Graeth, although I had mailed him several times. He had forgotten me, I thought sadly. For him, I was just another girl. He had led this life for years, while for me this was a unique period in my life, probably never to be repeated. I would have to go back to my studies in India, work towards scholarships, perhaps go to the United States where my cousins lived. I would have to think about a career, and also taking care of my father. Yes, this was the only space I had in which to experience the Image World, a short breathing space, too short ... too short, but all the more precious for this transience, and I wanted to live every drop, drink it to the dregs if I could.

There was a mail from Rukhsaar, my old roommate from Saint Anne's in Nainital. I was really surprised to see it. Rukhsaar and her husband, Anees Ali Khan, a cloth merchant, were going to be passing through Paris, and wanted to see me, of course. Imagine Rukhsaar, whom I had always considered a backward Muslim girl, in Paris! She would be here wearing her scarf, I supposed, and walk down the Champs Elysées, not eating any of the meat dishes in case they were not *halaal,* and buying the best perfumes which had been made from animals who had not been killed the *halaal* way, naturally. I would be happy to see her. An affection existed between us, having shared a room so many years. I had treated her badly at times, as she had me. But she had been very good when Rahul had been murdered, she had looked for me, found me, brought me back to the hostel, she had informed the nuns of my condition, she had wept for me. In the long run she had loved me better than I had loved her. She had considered me a bad Muslim, but had loved me nevertheless. She had understood my love for a Hindu boy, although she disapproved. Now after so many years I had begun to understand her. She was part of the sisterhood—the sisterhood to which, I, Marina, Agnès Desmoulins, Khadija, and Ferhat, we all belonged— and I had not loved her well.

Considering that Anees was minting money in his cloth business, which included bringing Banarasi silks and Kashmir silks and embroidery to Paris, we met for lunch at the Tour d'Argent, which I wouldn't otherwise have visited on my own. She looked the same Rukhsaar, but she was larger and rounder, no she wasn't expecting, she said, as she wrapped me in her arms. She was just happy with Anees and they were both getting fat. It was true. Anees was a stout man with a face too large for his body, kind eyes, and stubby hands. He didn't have a beard, as I had expected, fancying absurdly that Rukhsaar's husband had to be a typical orthodox Muslim, with all the trappings of beard, *surma* and *paijama.* I laughed at my childishness when I saw Anees. He was an ordinary man, a little shy, pink in the cheek, brown in the eye, like a characteristic Pathan, though not very tall, dressed in an ordinary T-shirt, jacket, and sports shoes, and Rukhsaar wasn't wearing a scarf either! She was in a *shalwar–kameez,* wearing an expensive jacket over it.

We ordered *aiguillettes de canard*, duck meat fingers with a side dish of potatoes *au gratin* and a tomato on top with green beans, and *canard à la presse*, the most famous mallard dish of the Tour d'Argent, and they never asked if it was *halaal.* Anees spoke a little broken French, as he did business with Frenchmen and thought it was necessary to know a little of the language.

Rukhsaar was delighted by the décor, which I thought was too flashy, and she told her husband she would like to have the miniature lamps that lit individual tables at her home too. They examined the lamps carefully, and he said he would get some made for her in Bareilly.

No, it wasn't the same Rukhsaar, I had been mistaken at first sight. She had evolved into a woman, the wife of a good man, for whom the petty considerations of outward religious symbols had taken a back seat. I was at once surprised and pleased by this change.

Rukhsaar wanted to know all about me and said she would love to see the apartment I lived in, but they didn't have the time. She wasn't in the least judgmental, in fact she sounded excited when I told her I was painting, and I was alone; she said she wished she could spend a few days with me in Montmartre.

I didn't see them again on that trip, as they were only there for two days and had to go on to London to see Anees' brother who lived in Chelsea. He had an English wife, Anees said. No, she hadn't converted, and the children were baptized Catholics.

They had brought back a whiff of home to me, and I felt a longing to return to India, to *Isfahan*, to my father, to Zehra *Phuphi*, and my grandparents. How cheerless the image of *Isfahan* seemed though, without the presence of my mother beside my father. How lonely he must be. I clutched this yearning inside me, and walked quickly, my head bent, to the metro Pont Marie. Thank God I wasn't an immigrant, I said gratefully to myself. I would go home.

9
Of the Unknowable

Isabelle came without her kids although it was her sister's birthday. She came in the morning, and Agnès had made a small raisin cake, just for us, as Dodi the Beloved had gone out with Manès Trigot, his Angel. From somewhere Agnès fished out an old guitar, and the sisters sat tuning it in the larger salon, talking of their childhood. Monsieur Desmoulins called, that was the first time in my presence that Agnès received a call from Skikda. He wished her, I suppose, and I heard her thank him, and say she had received the money. That she didn't need anything else. Her face took on a pinched look, but it soon disappeared, as we ate the cake she had prepared, and drank coffee. Just the four of us.

I had bought a bottle of wine and a small bouquet for Agnès. Marina had knit her a scarf for the winter. I do not know what Isabelle gave her, she had already opened the gift and put it away before I came in.

Once the guitar had been properly tuned, Isabelle and Agnès began to sing French songs, old classic ones, and of the seventies, when they had been young. From birthday songs they went to hymns, finally taking up the classic number from the sixties, "*Mon Amie La Rose,*", so beautifully, so plaintively, that it brought tears to my eyes and to theirs too. It had been their mother's favourite song, they said.

Believe, those who can, that I need Hope, without which I am nothing. Or such a brief something.

Vois le dieu qui m'a faite
M'a fait courber la tête.
Et je sens que je tombe.
Et je sens que je tombe
Mon coeur est presque nu
J'ai le pied dans la tombe.
Déjà je ne suis plus.
Tu m'admirais que hier et
Je serais poussière.
Pour toujours demain.

"See, the God who made me, makes me bow my head, and I feel I am falling, and I feel I am falling....my heart is almost naked, I have one foot in the tomb, already I am nothing. Only yesterday you admired me, and I shall be dust forever tomorrow...."

I had never heard it before, and it moved me deeply. Marina came from behind, and put her arm about my shoulder. It was a strange moment, a moment like a painting.

Isabelle, as she strummed the notes on the guitar, began telling me that their father had been in a travelling job, and they lived in the suburbs as children. She said their mother was a very special person, and she would take in stray cats and dogs, nurse injured birds back to health and bring in beggars to feed ... and she would always hum this song.Malko crawled in as she spoke, screeched in delight, and wanted to touch the guitar, and the spell was broken.

Isabelle had to go back before lunch. So she did not wait for Dodi to return, but they had a long discussion about his outings with Monsieur Trigot, that things seemed to be going well, except he was very reticent and wouldn't tell anyone where he went. He appeared much calmer too, and slept a lot. That seemed to worry Agnès, but Isabelle said it was probably a good thing.

Marina took me aside and said, "I don't know, but he seems to have the look on his face that my friends had when they smoked gum and polish back in Mezquital, in Guatemala. I don't dare tell Agnès. What will she think?"

I told her not to worry, we'd find out sooner or later if that were the case, and it wasn't her fault anyway. But I did not forget, for there was bound to be something in what she had said.

There would be no place for Agnès' past in my painting I knew, and the moment we had lived that morning had to remain outside of all those I culled for my work because in her past that sense of loss had not been there, the sense of loss that came with the birth of Dodi, with the departure of her husband, and ultimately with the departure of Emir.

***

I invited Bernardo and Anita for a cup of Indian tea. Bernardo said he wouldn't come if I did not show him my painting. So I agreed but on the condition that he would not ask me to explain what I had made; that would be difficult before it was completed, I said, and he agreed to that. I was no cook, but I told them I'd fry them some *pakoras* with onions and green chillies, as a snack with the tea. I was in fact thrilled they were coming over. I arranged some plum cake in a tray, and used Monsieur Houllebecq's deep frying pan to make the *pakoras*, and my two Italian friends were very generous in their appreciation.

Even before tea, Bernardo insisted the time had come to look at my painting. I steeled myself, and led them into the room where it stood, and removed the newspaper covering. I wanted to hide myself as I saw them look critically at my work. It was my first work, first work out of my head, and it was already so complicated!

Bernardo looked serious, "There's something there, there's something there," he articulated very slowly. "It's a gathering, or some momentous event. It is kind of surrealist, don't you think, *cara?*" he was talking to himself and to Anita. Then he asked me "The people in the painting... do they know each other?"

I was quiet. Did the people know each other? I had never thought of that. The question may also well be, did they know they were there? Some did, I responded uncertainly. The others of course were the "visitors", the travellers, the mourners, and in the second painting, there was Agnès's soul travelling across the Mediterranean, and Khadija's yearning spirit strung across the blue waters, and they both looked out, one with longing, and one with the scraping emptiness of the impuissance over her own life.Anita thought I should complete it and then she would like to see it again, she said. She too looked thoughtful, and I felt perhaps it was much too different from what people normally painted these days. I went now and then to the exhibitions at the Centre Georges Pompidou, and for the most part, contemporary art from all over Europe failed to touch me. Often it seemed to emanate from spirits that had not felt deeply enough. They were lacking in emotion, as Bernardo often said.

"If you want to sell art," said Bernardo, leaning heavily forward in the slim wooden chair, as we sat with our mugs of tea, "it must be what the public is expecting. If you do or say or write something beyond their ken, collectors, publishers, curators do not buy."

Anita sipped her tea, and chewed thoughtfully on her cake. "Art has become very selfish, it shows in the work. There is little brilliance, very little. Because the wish to sell has overtaken the wish to communicate. Everyone wants to be a sensation, everyone wants to be rich, famous, and they do not listen to the small things cooking inside them. They create art without thought, without love. "

Art is a commodity, the Pied Piper had said.

"And those who do listen for the little things cooking inside them, what happens to them? They struggle, for they are not showmen, they do their own thing, and they do not cater to the pulse of the public. It's not their job. Their job is to create." Bernardo added forlornly.

"Yet there were those like Dali, who believed he was the best, there were those like da Vinci, who were somewhat worldly wise, unlike Michelangelo."

"So many artists, writers, singers, musicians disappear ... no one remembers them, not because they were wanting in talent, but because they did not have the right platform."

We drank our tea in silence. I wondered if I had talent. If anything would come my way. If it mattered to me at all. I did not know. I knew only the things "cooking" inside me.

Bernardo suddenly brightened. "But should that make one sad? Life is to be lived, now, today. Not to be turned into a museum, not to become a mausoleum. How lucky are those who have talent, even a little. The man who plays the flute at the corner of the Sacré-Coeur, you, me, are we not happy? So what if the world will not remember us after we die? Should we therefore spend our lives in sorrow? We are alive, let us live, paint and be joyful! All destinies are not the same!"

He took Anita by the hand, and they thanked me, I thanked them, and Bernardo kissed me on the cheek and said "Bravo!"

After they left, I looked at *The Bereavement* once more. Was it surrealist? I had read in the books on Monsieur Houllebecq's shelves that surrealism was the dictate of dream and thought, over all reason, the continuity between the state of wakefulness and the state of slumber, of dreaming. Images that appear from the unconscious mind, outside of all moral or aesthetic concern.

Yes, there were definitely surreal elements. I thought how interesting it would be if I could give parts of it a mosaic effect — Agnès, consort of Emir of the Mediterranean, and Dodi, the Beloved, disappearing slowly, and emerging as Agnès Desmoulins, *parisienne,* with Jean-François, not-so-beloved; so that when you looked at the tableau from one angle, you would see one of the identities, and as you moved about the room the other identities would emerge, but I did not have the means to make such a painting, neither the technique nor the know-how. But that would be so real. That's what was happening in real life to these two persons.

Fabrice called to say he was going for a week to Tuscany with Jeannine, and I felt very uncomfortable. I did not ask if they were going on a holiday or on work. Tuscany, why? But he told me himself: they were going there in connection with an Italian cookbook, the author lived in Tuscany. I was only slightly relieved by this knowledge. I fought with myself. I had no right to be jealous. A kiss or two meant nothing. I was offering the man zilch. Not today, not tomorrow. That he called to tell me was kind of him. If I needed something, he said, he was still contactable at the same number.

Feeling suddenly *de trop* in his life, I took the metro to Trocadero. I would go to the Musée de l'Homme. "I am treasure, or tomb, depends on how you view me" that's roughly what it says on the museum building. I wanted to see the largest squid in the world, found by the Maoris. Something natural makes one feel normal. Even if it's a dead squid. But I decided first to eat an Italian ice and sit on the steps looking at the Tour Eiffel. A typical post-card-pretty Parisian view. I sat there for a while and then resolved to go in to see the giant squid after all, several times larger than a grown man, a dead grown man or a living grown man. That didn't matter, the squid was dead. A *Calmar plastiné.*

There is an anguish in Paris, a loneliness, a cold, clutching emptiness, a giant plasticized dead-squidness, which if you do not see, you can sit in the cafés and eat and drink and be merry, and visit the nightclubs, and buy perfumes at the Champs-Elysées, and take the train to Versailles to see the palace.

I thought Versailles the most insupportable palace I had ever seen. It looks good in pictures. There are too many sculptures. Too many pictures. There is no serenity. Only at the edge of the garden, before the fountain, if you lie down under the tall trees, it is restful. The people in the sculptures, the people in the pictures, all look caged, imprisoned. They do not lead to another dimension, these works of art. They are suffocating. Just stone, just paint. Fabrice had taken me to Versailles and had been surprised at my horror of it.

"Architecture, art, décor, must be a little spare; this is overdone."

He had laughed. He must have thought me a villager, but I couldn't retract my feelings about the place. It made me sick.

At that moment I found everything insupportable, and I hoped this wouldn't last the whole week that Fabrice was away.

To my delight, I became too busy that week to think about Fabrice. I found something terribly exciting to do, and I took Marina into confidence. That very day when I was returning from the museum I saw Dodi and Manès Trigot at the Place Charles Dullin, eating hotdogs off the temporary stall of a vendor who comes there some days. And who was with them? Dominique, the peroxide blonde of the spiritual tours! They were sitting on a bench. Who was standing beside them? Sukhi, and his brother, smoking those thin rolled up cigarettes, and they passed one to Dodi, who made an effort at inhaling the smoke, took a drag, coughed a bit, and the group laughed. I slipped quietly away, skirting the supermarket, so they didn't spot me.

I went straight up to my apartment, panting in my haste up the hill, and called Marina on the phone. Yes, she said she would come, as Mekel was asleep. Within a few minutes she was there. She said Agnès was waiting for Dodi. She was washing clothes in the washing machine, and was busy. I told her what I had seen.

"Do you think it could be … ?"

"Possibly something one smokes," said Marina.

The difficult part was to decide whether we should tell Agnès or not. Marina had lived with her now for several months, but she said there was a reticence in the French culture that she couldn't break through. She said it would be hard for her to be the carrier of such a tale, which may well be a tale for all we knew, to Agnès. I, in any case, was not in a position to intrude in their life. But I said before I left for India I would tell her … what difference would it make then?

We decided to wait a bit. Marina said she could check Dodi's belongings, as she often helped clean his room and his cupboard. Maybe she could find something there. About Manès Trigot, she said he did not look as though he drugged himself in any way.

Marina was preoccupied all of a sudden, as though her thoughts had shifted into another dimension. She played with the beaded strings at the edge of her dress, and her eyes clouded.

I said I would make some coffee, and she agreed to let me. When I returned from the kitchen with the coffee on a tray, she was still sitting in the same position.

"Is something the matter?" I asked

"If you don't talk about it to anyone, I can tell you."

"Of course, I wouldn't dream of it!" I said

"There's a young man. A Spaniard I met at the shops; he works here. His name is Lorenzo too, by coincidence. He does not earn a very big salary. He works for a courier company. But he said we could get married and live in one of the HLM outside Paris, if we wanted. We could be happy."

"Will he adopt Malko?" was my first thought.

"Yes, that's what he says."

"Are his papers in order?"

"He's Spanish, from Andalusia. From a place called Murcia. He has a work permit. He said we could go back there someday after we'd earned a bit of money. His mother has a house which she will give him, he says."

"You have to check him out, Marina", I said, worried now.

"You know, it was like music, to hear Spanish spoken, and the name Lorenzo, it called out to me of its own, and I remembered our journey in the truck, and all the days of hardship on the ship aboard in which the first Lorenzo had seen me…and then left me."

"But have you told Madame Desmoulins?"

"No," she said "How can I tell her? What can I tell her? That I am planning to leave? After all her kindnesses?"

"But Marina, if you leave with him, what is the guarantee that he will take care of you? And if he does not care for your Malko, what then?" I had heard her stories of men abandoning women, and they had scared me, for her. Perhaps for myself too.

She sighed. "I don't think I will have the courage to depend on a man again, *hermana.* But inside me there is a longing, for I am still young, am I not? Longing for a home of my own, for a husband, for the arms of a man. Do you not have these longings, *hermana*?"

"Not for any man, Marina, but if there is a man I like, maybe I will long for him. The man I longed for is dead now."

"But all of us have this need, to find our way. I long for the large spreading trees of Guatemala, for the birds I never hear in Paris, the heat, the rhythms of the drums, the colours; now I have to live this tictoctictoctictoc-greygreygrey…my body has forgotten me, I have forgotten my body. But when I meet Lorenzo, the sound of my name on his lips awakens me; I am no longer asleep to my needs. Oh Meyjumbee, oh, *hermana*… can I be so villainous, so treacherous, to all those who have saved me from a terrible fate?"

I was indeed alarmed. Here, after a tumultuous childhood and youth, she seemed to finally have a secure life for herself and her child, and she was drawn towards insecurity once more. We had to wait, I told her. Lorenzo or no Lorenzo, she must think about Mekel first. Could Lorenzo provide him the life he could have in Paris as a protégé of Agnès and her sister? He had the opportunity of getting the best education, and becoming one day an engineer, a doctor, but with Lorenzo he would have to struggle, struggle struggle … and who knows Lorenzo may not prove to be such a good father? I put all these arguments to her, hoping she would get swayed.

It was that her only sanctuary, both financial and emotional, lay with Madame Desmoulins. Lorenzo's love and commitment were debatable. And if that is what she really wanted, to be with Lorenzo, then surely it would have to be discussed with Madame Desmoulins? For poor Marina, a very difficult situation had developed.

I said I should like to meet Lorenzo. Perhaps he could be introduced to Madame Desmoulins initially as someone who was known to me? Neither Marina nor I relished the idea of fooling Agnès. We decided it was better for her to wait awhile. In the meantime I would like to meet Lorenzo, I said, and she did not see it as an intrusion.

***

Leave, we must all leave, I thought. Graeth had left, Anita and Bernardo would leave, and even Marina would leave. There was something that drove us all towards different destinies. My father had once shown me a caterpillar in an old shoe in the potting shed.

He had picked it up and taken it far away down the garden and left it under the trees. A few hours later it was back. It must have had a destiny to fulfil.

I had to leave too, and it was because of all the people waiting for me back in India, at *Isfahan*, our home. But Agnès and Dodi? They would not leave, even though Agnès wanted to. They would stay here forever, going up and down the hill of Montmartre, under the white shadow of the Sacré-Coeur, *tictoctictoctictocgrisgrisgris* …

I was walking down to the post office the next morning, to collect the money transfer my father had made, when I bumped into a man coming from the other direction; it was George Washington of Sierra Leone, of the friendship bands. He was very cordial, and shook my hand, having immediately recognized me. He told me he had found a job in a supermarket near the Bibliothèque François Mitterrand, and was just visiting his friends in Montmartre. He looked clean and smart and self-assured. He told me also, tongue-in-cheek, that he didn't want me for a *petite amie* any more, as he'd found one for himself, a young receptionist from Tunis, who worked part time at a hotel and who wrote poetry. I was surprised he'd remembered our conversation, which I hadn't forgotten as it had been an unusual experience for me. *Bayou-bayou-haramba!*

"My name is Mohammed Jhalloh", he said, as a parting shot, and he smiled. My mood lifted. Here was one person at least, in no hurry to leave. He was happy being wherever he was.

I went to the Taxiphone service by the Abbesses to mail Daddy, to tell him I had received the money. I found I had mail from Graeth in my inbox! I opened it before I did anything else, so excited was I.

There were but few lines on the page:

Chère amie,

"In the human being there is the unknowable, which is linked to his very Liberty, and because of which he cannot be

caught in (thus escapes) the logic of causal determinism"

—Montesquieu

The universe is governed by determinism if, and only if, given a specified way things are at a time t, the way things go thereafter is fixed as a matter of natural law. The roots of determinism were sown by Leibniz in what he called the Principle of Sufficient Reason.

Bises,

Graeth

It was a profound communication to me, however impersonal it may have appeared to a third person. He seemed to know what I was seeking. He seemed to be reading my mind. But then, he was the Pied Piper.

Someone else too, someone as eminent as Montesquieu, had said there was the unknowable in the human being. I wasn't being a fool after all, when I was following my intuition about the painting. The unknowable in each person must obviously be different, otherwise it wouldn't be unknowable. (Dodi and I, though, seemed to have similar unknowables!)

And determinism? Didn't I believe that we are the way we are because of the way *were*, and that we shall be the way we shall be because of what we *are*? It seemed logical enough to me. So where was the space for the unknowable? Inspiration? Alternate realities? Optional existences?

But it is the Unknowable in us that knows the Unknowable that reveals to us truths otherwise unknowable.

Also there was the very *arbitrariness* of certain things; perhaps because they were so small, they had no place in the larger scheme. (Like a man lifting a caterpillar and placing it far away from the chosen shoe.) Then finally there was *chaos,* chaos I couldn't integrate in my reasoning.

Were one to predict by this logic Marina's decision, she would follow Lorenzo. I considered she had Sufficient Reason to do so.

***

Now our attention was divided between Dodi's predicament, and Marina's dilemma. Both were important. Without Marinas' help we could never find out what Dodi and Manès Trigot were up to.

It was Marina who took the lead and came up with all the ideas.

Marina would stroll down to Dominique's dark little shop. She said she would speak only Spanish, she wouldn't let on that she lived in Montmartre. She would go there a few times and sit around languidly, pretending to be stoned; she knew well how to do that. She knew well the demeanour of persons on heroin too. (If the police came around she would immediately change her deportment). She would wear an old *huipil* she had, and not brush her shining long hair. She would carry my dollars. It all sounded easy enough.

She brought it in a brown-paper bag, her *huipil,* to show to me its colours woven in cotton in a large geometric floral design with the traditional sun around the neck; it lay upon my bed, reflecting a life and a time unimaginable in Paris. It spoke not only of aesthetic splendour, not only of the stories of the ancient Mayas; it spoke of the oppressed and the disinherited living surrounded by insecurity and violence. Of State repression.

Marina saw me looking at it. "We are poor and humble, say the Mayas", she said "But we are not incapable. We represent ideas through our art; we use art as a weapon against subjugation."

Riot police, evictions from lands that were their homes, spiritual as well as physical, massacre of the indigenous inhabitants, repressed and marginalized by light skinned European people—they were left with nothing but their art to exist in. Colours and forms spoke of a history that could not be obliterated, spoke of the human spirit that could not be suppressed. Art was a refuge, a spiritual space, a means of continuance, a weapon. How meaningful such art was compared to anything I could ever create ….

Marina said she would carry the *huipil* in a bag up to a point then wear it over her clothes at an opportune moment, and go to Dominique's shop. She said over the week she would find out whether and exactly which kinds of drugs were available at Dominique's.

That night, I awoke from a dream in which words and colours and geometrical patterns spun around each other—Mezquital, nahuales, Chimaltenango, Quetzal, Ixil, Maximon—-my heart was thudding with the unknown rhythms of these words. I tore the newspaper off my painting, and brought out my paints, the rug on the floor in *The Bereavement of Agnès Desmoulins* took on the shades and designs of Marina's *huipil.*

10
ABSINTHE

Even before Marina's first excursion, Fabrice returned from Italy. He called and said I was being invited to a very unusual party, and that I mustn't refuse, although it may be against my ideology. I immediately imagined a sexual orgy, and my Indian middle class morality made me cringe inside; and I was ashamed of my backwardness, and I was afraid of my fear itself; I was afraid to say no and I was afraid to say yes, but Fabrice resolved my panic by saying we were going to a party where something very special to drink was being served.

It was a drizzly evening as usual, and Fabrice met me after office hours at La Madeleine, to where I could get a direct metro from Abbesses. We walked down to the venue as it wasn't far from the metro station, Fabrice said. He took my hand, and I was happy. The gathering was at the Rue du Faubourg Saint-Honoré, in a little flat, several floors up. We climbed by a creaking, narrow, wooden, spiral staircase. We entered a dimly lit room, very large indeed in proportion to the stairway. The windows were large too, but the blinds were drawn, and only a little of the light from the evening entered the room. Michel Sardou was blaring on the music deck, his wonderful emotional voice singing "The River of our Childhood": "*Ce n'est pas le sang qui coule dans nos veines, c'est la rivière de notre enfance*"… It's not blood that flows in our veins; it's the river of our childhood.

About a dozen young people, in their twenties and thirties crowded the room, but they were apparently waiting for more to arrive. They were mostly white and not all French for I could hear snatches of British English and Spanish. There were also two or three tall black men, no black women. People were smoking and a lot of jollity filled the air, but no one as yet was drinking anything. Jeannine was there too and she came and kissed me on both cheeks and kissed Fabrice on the mouth even though he was holding my hand.

There was an enlarged print of Edgar Degas' oil on canvas, *L'Absinthe* in a prominent place on the largest wall. It was obvious it had just been put there as it was stuck with pins on the sides. The doped-looking woman in the hat in the painting was the actress Ellen Andrée and the man was Marcellin Desboutin, a painter and engraver. The café was the Parisian Café de la Nouvelle Athènes. A little note on the side explained that.

Many absinthe posters from the Belle Epoque were displayed on the walls, including the famous one by Frederic Christol, from 1910 with "*L'alcool, voila l'Ennemi*" (Alcohol, here's the enemy!) written in big red letters over an absinthe bottle that has a skull made on it with "Poison" written below it, and a group of people looking at it curiously. There was even a dog in the picture. Another small note at the edge explained the poster's history.

A print of Picasso's *Bouteille de Pernod et Verre* hung alongside a print of the famous chromolithograph which I believe used to hang in every cafe in Paris at one time. They told me a copy of this poster based on a painting by Charles Maire, had hung in Picasso's studio during the time when he was producing his early cubist work.

Picasso had given his copy to Jean Cocteau apparently, as a gesture of friendship. Also on the wall were photographs of Picasso's sculptures of the absinthe glass, *Verre d'Absinthe.* Other smaller prints of works by Van Gogh, Braques, and Toulouse-Lautrec were pinned about the room, almost covering the wallpaper

A polished wooden bar, with drawers on one side, held many Pontarlier style reservoir glasses, straight out of the lithograph, and several bottles of Absinthe, all different makes and types. I could see through the glass an assortment of very decorative perforated spoons, like leaves with holes in them and elongated stalks.

A few minutes after our arrival the door was flung open and a young woman in a flowing green chiffon dress, with a high Roman nose and dark long hair, burst into the room. From the way she entered and began to bustle about, I guessed she was the hostess, and I learnt her name was Karen. She was a freelance illustrator and graphics artist, and one of the best. She worked with several top publishers.

"*La fée verte est entrée,*" someone said. Fabrice told me that absinthe was called the green fairy, *la fée verte*.

She had with her three or four large pastry boxes full of eats and she began to lay them out on a table near the door. There was antipasto in separate paper plates for each person wrapped in cellophane: chorizo sausage, salt and pepper calamari, and smoked salmon. The oysters were separate, and there was millefeuille, with pesto as well as with chocolate! There were also lemon tarts and breads and cheeses of various kinds.

"Eat," said Karen in a commanding voice, "especially all those who don't have a good head for alcohol." She smiled at me, as though she knew I didn't. Fabrice said I must eat something, and there were others who did too.

Karen switched off the player.

"This party, for me, is very special," she said after getting everyone's attention. "Absinthe is no longer banned, it's been a while, but now many kinds of brands are available. You can choose yours. This was the favourite drink of some of my favourite artists! It's now made in such a way that there's very little alcohol as compared to what those *mecs* used to drink. Personally I prefer anisefree absinthe, but a lot of people like it with anise and fennel, and I do too, sometimes; now we're going to perform the ritual as it should be done in the correct French way, and I shall drink it in front of you to show you it's not going to kill you!"

Karen went into the kitchen and emerged with a jug of cold water filled with ice cubes, and an outsize sugar-bowl with large-sized sugar cubes. "I don't have a *brouilleur*, *pardon!* "

A hush fell on the gathering as Karen selected one of the reservoir glasses, and one of the perforated leaf-like spoons, and put them on a low table before her. She took out a bottle of absinthe from the bar: it read "Pernod" on the green bottle. Pouring a small amount of the greenish liquid into the glass, Karen took a large lump of sugar from the sugar pot and placed it in the spoon. She balanced the spoon across the glass, and slowly, caressingly, began to drip the iced water over the sugar. In a while the liquid in the glass started to cloud over. The party clapped and hooted and whistled.

"*Voila, ça louche*!" said a man

"*Tu es louche, toi!*" cried another to him. There was general laughter. Fabrice explained louche meant "cloudy" and also "suspect", if used for a person. Good quality absinthe would always louche.

"Knock knock" said an American

"Who's there?"

"Claude".

"Claude who?"

"Claude Lelouch!"

"Ha", giggled a British girl, "you are *Clod* Le Louche!"

Karen picked up the glass and sipped the drink, a delighted expression on her face.

"*C'est délicieux*!" she cried ecstatically. There was general clapping. A Spanish fellow came forward and grabbed a glass; he put the sugar cube as Karen had done in the spoon, but instead of pouring the absinthe into the glass, he poured it directly over the sugar and then lit it with a match. It burned with a greenish yellow flame, and there were sighs from everyone. The party had begun in earnest now. I was hoping no one would offer me a drink, but then, as was to be expected, Fabrice brought me a glass, that smelled of aniseed, and when I tasted it I thought it rather nice, though a bit bitter.

"To wormwood!" cried a girl as she raised her glass.

I went to the bar to look at the different kinds of the alcohol, green, and red and bleu too—Verte de Fougerolles, Chateau Ferran, Spanish absinthe, Staroplzenecky, Czech, Bairnsfather *bitter*, German, Partisane, Roquette, François Guy—all French. It was fascinating. I sipped the liquid very slowly, as usual scared.

The company continued to make jokes, "Bairnsfather, *bitte*," said one, when asked what he wanted, but after a while, after a few drinks each, different expressions began to fit themselves onto their heretofore clear faces. There was cloudiness in their eyes, also happiness. The guests began to drift off to various parts of the apartment; no one seemed to care any longer. Someone was singing, and no one bothered to play any more music. Someone opened the windows and the noise of the traffic on the road came inside in a big rush with the cold air.

Fabrice sat close to me. He said in my ear, "Oscar Wilde said, when you drink absinthe, after the first glass, you see things as you wish they were. After the second, you see things as they are not. Finally, you see things as they really are, and that is the most horrible thing in the world."

"I don't need absinthe," I said boldly, "I see things as they are, Fabrice, when I want. When I don't want, I see things as I wish them to be, although somewhere I know it's not the truth. And I am also capable of seeing things as they are not in real life."

"Brave words," smiled Fabrice, "Give me an example."

I think something of the liquor must have affected me. "For example," I said, "sometimes I pretend to myself you love me, sometimes I know that you don't, and sometimes I pretend I love you."

He put his arms around me and his lips to mine. "There is no truth and no fancy that can match up to this," he said, "Flesh against flesh. That's the ultimate truth."

I pushed him away gently, in a mood for argument, "No, Fabrice, this too is a lie, a dream. Sometimes we are not, when we are, and sometimes when we are, we are not."

A man called Edouard joined us, and spoke to Fabrice in rapid French. Fabrice laughed, and went off with him to get more of the absinthe he was drinking.

I didn't know where Jeannine had gone, I didn't see her, although I was looking out for her, especially when Fabrice made to hold and kiss me. Maybe she saw, maybe she left. I felt sorry. But Fabrice seemed quite content without her. It was strange.

I had another glass; I tried Czech this time, and I couldn't really tell the difference. I knew I was happy, inordinately happy, and I was letting Fabrice caress my cheeks..

Everything had shadows and interior spaces that had become visible to me. The beauty of beautiful things made my heart ache, the flowers on the cushions, the wrought iron railing, the cream lampshade with light falling out of it like yellow cream, all seemed to me infinitely beautiful. The blue and white design on Fabrice's cotton shirt was so exquisite, his red pullover with the yellow self designed flowers across the chest so heart-warming, made by a labour of love; Fabrice's fingers appeared so familiar, and so dear; everything seemed perfectly in accord, the way the chairs sat around the room, the angle at which the panes were open, the angle at which the light of the street-lamp fell onto the floor, the red and blue neon of the hoarding across the street: everything seemed as it should be, put there by a divine hand in a divine harmony, like a perfect symphony playing silently, moving gently and palpably towards a celestial destiny—here *was* the Other World.

Before they left, the guests had all been gifted a tiny sample-bottle of absinthe *verdoyante* and it was this bottle that lay on my pillow when I awoke the next morning. I had no memory of how I had got back; whether Fabrice had dropped me, or, I had taken the metro, my mind drew a blank. But a certain joy of the experience of beauty remained with me, something warm and soft and glowing. And the song, "*Ce n'est pas le sang qui coule dans nos veines …*" the River of our Childhood, played in my head.

I was in love with life. I was in love with Paris. I was in love with Fabrice.

***

Marina knocked at my door about ten a.m. She was surprised to see me so groggy. I told her I'd been to an absinthe party. Her eyes shone. "At last!" she said, "You have found the courage to enjoy yourself! One has to live life, *hermana,* otherwise it will just pass by, and we are then left with nothing. And in Paris, what is there to stop you? What threatens you except excess? I am sure you are sensible enough."

She seemed renewed, almost transformed, and I thought it was because of her new beau, Lorenzo. And because she had told me about him, she was happier. I dressed and made coffee for both of us. Mekel was playing with Madame Desmoulins, she was getting more and more attached to him as the days passed. He had become more responsive now as he became older and his health improved. That drew Agnès to him.

"He was such a mite when I came, such a miserable mite!" Marina said. "He had forgotten to smile, so malnourished he was."

She looked thoughtful, and then looked at me meaningfully and said, "We must leave the Past where it belongs. Behind us."

I regarded her attentively; did we want to leave the Past behind? Why then were the Three Breaths of Life, a reminder of one's ancestors, given to a newborn? Did the Past leave us, even if we wanted to disengage ourselves from it?

The world is surrounded by threads of Time, of the Past, of the Present, of the Future; millions, billions, trillions of them wound around and around the earth. We can but follow one thread in one life, the thread that leads each individual from birth until death. In one time, in one dimension. But the times past and the times to come, those that lived and those that are yet to live, are all there, present, unseen and unknown to each other, following their respective threads, in their respective time planes, around and around, as the world spins around the sun, and the sun moves in the galaxy and the galaxies move in the ever-expanding universe … bigger and smaller, before and after, all relatively.

I don't know why I thought these thoughts; the effect of the absinthe must still be present, somewhere, but I didn't believe the Past lets you go. Paris *was* the Past *and* the Present *and* the Future; it was, although it was strange. All the clocks melted when you came to Paris and became involved in its time warp. Nerval still lived at the Folie Sandrin, and at the Allée des Brouillards ; Dali lived here, and Toulouse-Lautrec, as did Amélie Poulain, as did Marina, maybe even Monsieur Séguin and his goats, the real and the fictional, all together. I did too, in a bubble of transience.

Marina said she was ready to go to the Rue des Trois Frères, to the blonde woman's shop, I said I'd wait for her by the post office, as I had some work there. She left and I settled the apartment, peered long and hard at my paintings, now two, and brought out my paints. I created a mist around Khadija, and placed a glass of glowing green liquor on the window sill, a clear stem glass; the liquor would flow out and mingle with the blue of the Mediterranean: *Something leads you to where you want to go; sometimes you cannot find the way alone, and something must steer you, something must guide you.*

I had barely left the building, and was going in the direction of the post office when I saw Marina running towards me. She had sprinted all the way up the hill, it appeared, as she was panting heavily.

"I came back!" she said "He was there, so I ran back before he could see me!"

"Who?" I asked, "Manès Trigot?"

"Yes, Monsieur Trigot, early in the morning! If he had seen me he would have known I was spying on him! So I ran back as quickly as I could."

"Let's go buy some juice at the store," I suggested, "then we can sit somewhere and talk".

"I have to go back, Mekel must be troubling Madame Desmoulins," she said

I let her go and proceeded to the *Poste.* The old Polish lady who opened the door recognized me by now and didn't ask me for a tip, only smiled. She knew I was no rich tourist. I couldn't talk to her at all, as we shared no common tongue. It was as if we were both dumb and deaf: we only smiled and nodded at each other every time.

11
The Snail and the Angel

A week passed and Fabrice did not call. I was always loath to ring his cell, as I thought he might be busy, and I would interrupt his work. I was too involved with Marina's and Dodi's tribulations to be missing him, although at the absinthe party I had felt very close to him, and I thought I might long for him the way I did one night not so long ago. But it did not happen. I was sleeping well, and feeling very healthy. The French food suited me, even if I ate simple meals of muesli and soups, cheeses, especially camembert, and baguette or *pain de seigle* which I didn't always relish except with the number of *Bonne Maman* preserves that I bought incessantly at the supermarket. I also ate a lot of butter with the cheese and bread, but Marina said I was too thin. Turkey ham and chicken sausages too filled the little refrigerator in Monsieur Houllebecq's kitchen. As did lettuce and tomatoes and olives. Peaches and apples. Then there were the flavoured fruity yoghurts, the *petit-suisses*, the cream chocolate puddings, and everything sweet, and bottles and bottles of juices. Food had begun to spell happiness for me. Daddy was sending me enough money, and I thanked him each time from my heart. I didn't want to buy anything or eat in expensive places; I wanted to paint and nibble and walk, walk and nibble, and paint. My dear, dear Daddy!

I gave Fabrice a missed call the eighth day. He called back immediately, and apologized for his neglect, he had been down with *la grippe,* influenza. I was contrite, regretting my own selfishness, and my vacillation. It was I could not be a friend to him, because of all my own irresolution and uncertainty where he was concerned. He was crystal clear in his mind as to what he wanted from me. He was also responsible in temperament. But then what he wanted would in no way alter his reality, but if I complied with his desires, my whole world would change and my reality would be disturbed beyond a point from which I may not be able to recover. And I did not want that.

Fabrice lived with his parents in a small suite of rooms that had its own balcony, its own entrance and its own bathroom. He ate his meals with his parents whenever they ate at home, which was often, for Paris, he said. He said more and more young French men and women were opting to remain within the family as long as they were not married. Parents were no longer demanding or authoritative, and it was a pleasant way of solving monetary difficulties too, although he himself had none. If the relationship worked, then the parents' old age loneliness in addition was solved by this arrangement. It was because their home, like most Parisian flats was private and small, that Fabrice hadn't ever invited me there, he said. His parents were hard working people and always surrounded with work, manuscripts, contracts, and often, lawyers. It really didn't matter to me. I was sure I would feel quite out of place in their home. At Vésinet-le-Pêque, they had been charming to me, and I think that was kind enough, I did not expect more. The Parisians are not apologetic for not inviting you home, it's their way of life; they prefer to meet you outside. Sometimes if they do invite you, they will offer you mineral water, or maximum a cup of tea, and rarely regale you with a feast like Rezwan and Ferhat had done at Aubervilliers.

***

Fabrice said he would meet me over the weekend as he had a lot of work to catch up on at the office, after his week-long absence. I was agreeable to this. A lack of expectation is so soothing to a friendship. I expected neither love nor fidelity; neither time nor gifts. What he gave me was far beyond my expectations, and I was happy to receive his friendship or love for whatever they were.

If I did not know the Desmoulins, I would have been lonely in Paris, and I would have left sooner, much sooner. But there they were, right across the courtyard, a family unlike any other I had known, bringing an unexpected richness to my life, and inspiring my art.

I called Marina, and we met in the quadrangle an hour later when Mekel had been put into his crib for his midday nap. Marina had her *huipil* in the brown bag. After a bit of consultation together, I took the Rue Foyatier and she went straight down to the Rue des Trois Frères, to Dominique's shop. I strolled down the steps, imagining Dodi's past and Mekel's future, then turned right towards the Square Charles Dullin. To my surprise I saw Marina talking animatedly to a young man with very black hair and moustaches. He wore a smart yellow T-shirt, blue jeans and white keds. I reached them presently, little out of breath, and he smiled a rather pleasant white smile at me. I had guessed correctly that this must be Lorenzo. The three of us walked down to one of the cafés on the Boulevard de Rochechouart, a seedy one, and Lorenzo elaborated on his plans for himself and Marina. He was indeed very attractive, and looked earnest and convincing, but I noticed that when he had to pay for our coffees he hesitated, and looked at me for a split second, waiting to see if I would pay. I paid for mine and let him pay for Marina and himself. That small slip made me realize that it was possible he was not financially the person Marina should look to; he would make a fine boyfriend, perhaps lover, but considering Marina's precarious position in French society, he was conceivably the wrong choice of husband.

Lorenzo came in useful in our pursuit of Dominique's wares; we explained our quest to him, not letting on about Dodi or M. Trigot, and he said it wasn't a problem for him at all, he would just go and ask if she had any hashish, marijuana … what was it we wanted?

I didn't know if I should invite Lorenzo to my apartment, so he could meet Marina there, whether I should indeed play gooseberry, whether it was safe for me. However my good sense gave way to my sympathy for the couple and I told him he was welcome to meet Marina at my place. He took my number and gave me a long look, his eyes were not completely dark, considering his hair was jet black, and I felt a shiver run down my spine. Silly me, I thought.

The next time we met, however, was at the carrousel at Abbesses, he was making a call at the local phone booth and I was passing by to the Taxiphone service. He saw me and waved in a friendly way. He came out of the booth and walked up to me quickly.

"She has everything you want," he said. "But there are certain conditions she puts."

"Who?" I asked, wondering what it was I had wanted.

"You wanted some marijuana, right?"

"Ah!" I cried, "Okay, I know what you mean. No, actually it wasn't for me, it was just something I wanted to know."

"You don't have to be shy of me," he smiled in a way I didn't like. "I don't have any reservations about it."

"You don't understand…" I began. But I shut up, and threw one at him to change the subject and discomfit him in turn "Do you really think you can take care of Marina?"

"*Touché*!" he said and laughed, throwing back his head. "Yes, I knew the marijuana wasn't for you! And yes, I will, and can, take care of Marina. I love her. She is an amazing girl. I love children too. She will have more with me; Mekel will be our first child."

I really did not know what to make of him, but if Marina liked him there was nothing for me to say in the matter. I still felt, however, that she should not decide in haste, the security she had with the French in their own country was what she and her child needed, I could see that, however young I may have been at that juncture. For Marina, I could see it, from the outside. I do not know how, in her situation, I would have reacted myself.Now that we knew Dominique's little spiritual tours boutique did have other materials to soothe the spirit and the loneliness of troubled minds, what were we going to do about it? Were we sure that Manès Trigot was teaching Dodi to smoke hash, marijuana? We had no proof. I thought if I asked Sukhi, he might be able to throw some light on the matter. So early one morning I traipsed down the hill to the Square Charles Dullin where Sukhi and his brother slept and peed, early enough to catch Sukhi just as he awoke on the pavement.

I had with me some sandwiches of smoked chicken ham and some Danone desserts, which I offered him, and which he couldn't refuse, so destitute was he, living off the kindness of strangers after being fooled and deserted by his uncle. But when I questioned him he was evasive. I spoke earnestly in Hindi, appealing to his Indianness, our common origins, and it took me a while, but he thawed ultimately, quarrelled violently with his brother for a time in Punjabi, and chased him off rudely. When the younger one had gone, Sukhi told me the half-wit boy did come around once in a while with his diminutive friend and they smoked with him. No, not the short Frenchman, only the half-wit smoked. They sometimes paid him for a drag or two, not buying any of their own. But the half-wit still hadn't learnt how to take a drag properly; sometimes he could, and then the very next day he had forgotten how. This made Sukhi laugh, and I noticed how nice he looked when cheerful.

I thanked him, and told him I wouldn't bother him anymore. He settled down to a sad reverie on his tattered sleeping bag, and was slowly spooning the Danone into his unwashed mouth as I left.

When I returned to our building, the sun was out and I met Marina in the courtyard, walking little Malko in the sunshine.

"Where have you been so early, *hermana?*" she asked, surprised to see me.

I told her what I had learnt, and she was troubled. She said she would tell Agnès, but I knew she wasn't sure.

Agnès emerged from inside and stood in the doorway wishing me cheerily. The sun was on her face and you couldn't see the lines at all, and she looked young and untroubled. It was a Sunday, she said, she was preparing lunch already as Manès Trigot and Dodi would go off on an excursion, outside Paris perhaps, and she wanted to pack them something nice. She said she was eternally grateful to Monsieur Trigot who took out so much of his precious time to help her with Dodi.

I wondered what his profession was, and I asked. He was a consultant architect, she said, and also a realtor. He had many clients, important clients, he had told her. He had his offices in Paris and Fontainebleau, he said, but his wife, who had always been delicate in health, had died of pneumonia two winters ago, and his parents lived in Brussels, so he was lonely and liked to help people.

It was perhaps unkind of me, but I felt no twinge of sympathy for the man with the swivelling wrists, my prejudice against him having taken root quite firmly in my mind. I nodded, but all the time I was making mental pictures of Dodi being taken to smoke hashish.

"I don't know why you trust him so much," I blurted out, to

my own surprise. "I think you should at least find out if everything he says is true! Maybe he never had a wife!"

"Ah, Meyjumbee, you should not be of so much *mauvaise foi*!" Agnès said reprovingly, chiding my lack of faith. "I have always had experience of people who hardly know one and who are so helpful."

"Yes," I said, not wanting to press the issue yet, "Like I have you and Marina, and Marina has you, but …"

At this moment Mekel, who had waddled up to Agnès, smiled engagingly at her, and tried to climb onto her lap. Her face lit up, her attention diverted to him completely, and the conversation was forgotten. I looked at Marina, and she held up her hand reassuringly. Perhaps she meant she would speak to Agnès herself.

The sun disappeared, and in its absence the wind swooped down in devilish gusts and bit into our skin and we hurried indoors, I to my room. Khadija still had to be worked upon, and I hastily swallowed a cup of chocolate milk and brought out my paints. The chocolate milk tasted like medicine and I grimaced to myself.

Khadija was too sharply outlined; longing is muted, mitigated, and hazy. I mixed blue and grey and began to merge her garments with the colours of the sea she looked out upon, and the glass of green liquid that sat by her side, the liquid flowing out to recreate the world.

I couldn't get Dodi off my mind, because I couldn't do anything just yet. Who would believe the tale of a vagabond illegal *de trop* Indian, Sukhi, against a well settled Frenchman? Because I couldn't do anything, I took a coat and scarf to shield me against the biting wind, and went down to the Espace Montmartre to the Dali museum.

Every time I went there I was torn by pangs of envy. I wished I could be as confident, as self–assured, as uncaring of what people thought, as Salvador Felipe Jacinto Dali had been. I wanted to be able to say, like he had,

"Every morning when I wake up, I experience an exquisite joy—the joy of being Salvador Dalí—and I ask myself in rapture: What wonderful things this Salvador Dalí is going to accomplish today?"

He was considered the foremost surrealist painter, but it was I that dreams confused eternally. When I woke up I barely thought of Mehjabeen, everything around seemed bigger than her, including her painting, and the characters, the sounds, the colours, the shapes, that peopled her dreams at night. She had to get out of bed and creep into the surroundings to begin existing again. I, too, experienced that "irrational knowledge", based on the "delirium of interpretation" as Dali put it, but I thrust it aside, considering it of little practical value. The age of surrealism was long over. It had been discarded, as a method, put away into the past.

Nevertheless, going to the museum inspired me, as it did Dodi. I was afraid we were alike in many ways, Dodi, the Beloved, and I, Meyjumbee, although I would never have admitted it openly. Carriers of irrational knowledge.

My cellphone buzzed, and I knew it would be Fabrice, as he'd said we would get together on Sunday afternoon. I said I'd meet him at the Jardin du Luxembourg at four, at the small gate towards the Sénat. He said we'd walk around the Saint Germain area, and then he'd take me out to dinner on the Île Saint-Louis or the Quartier Latin. I was happy: his voice was now the voice of a friend, someone dearer to me than before.

My day ahead of four still hung before me like a melted clock on a wall. Anita and Bernardo had gone to Bretagne. I went to the cybercafé to check my mail and write to Daddy. I had a mail from Monsieur Houllebecq. He said he wouldn't return until the middle of the next month and I could stay on in his apartment if I wanted. He also invited me to visit him, if I so desired, and he would ask

Fabrice to drive me up to the little village where he spent his summer, Peille, in the Maritime Alps. I was utterly delighted by his charming proposal, and I hoped fervently that Fabrice would find the time. I would discuss it with him that very afternoon, or during dinner.

I reached the Luxembourg garden at three. I thought I would stroll around a bit before meeting Fabrice. There was to be a performance by a school band that had come all the way from England. The children were there at the covered concert area, the *kiosque à musique,* tuning their instruments, laughing and chatting. They were dressed in their school uniforms, so much like mine had been at Saint Anne's in Nainital. White shirts, red and green Scottish checks for the skirts and trousers, striped neckties.

There was also an exhibition of blow ups of photographs of malnourished children over the world, it was on the outside on the high green grills that demarcated the boundary of the garden towards the Sénat. I decided to go along the grills on the inside, where in the shrubbery there are several sculptures. The Grotto, commissioned by Marie de Medicis, second wife of Henri the Fourth, (Madame Desmoulins' ancestors came during that time to France too, in the seventeenth century). The Italian Queen, it was said, had wanted a reminder of her home town Florence, of the sculptures of the Boboli Gardens. Each one of us is tied by invisible strings to a place called "home", I thought to myself.

There is a lot of shrubbery on the inside of the grill, and on most days visitors prefer to enjoy the sunshine near the lake, to sit out under the trees on the green chairs. You will find very few people walking on the side of the sculptures. Somehow I took that inner lane along the grill. There was no one there, it was eerie, almost. The greenery is thick around the grotto, you can hear the birds in the foliage, and the sounds from the garden get dimmed as you pass. I thought I'd hasten my pace to avoid lingering too long on that lonely stretch, but at one point my eyes fell on a pair of legs sticking out from under a leafy bush. The heavy yellow shoes looked oddly familiar. In spite of myself I slowed my steps and peered, bending ever so slightly. Yes, it *was* Dodi, his eyes shut tight, still as a mannequin, and lying almost on top of him kissing his lips, caressing his chest and thighs with one square, white, swivelly hand was Manès Trigot! I nearly let out a scream of surprise, from an odd constricting feeling that suddenly gripped the middle of my chest. It was as if my heart had stopped for one moment and my breath caught in my throat. I felt as though I had been struck a hefty blow, then I was running, running away from the scene as fast as I could, not along the path but across the ground, through and over bushes, towards the other gate where I was to meet Fabrice.

My mind seemed to be bursting… images, sounds, words, all crowding in, plummeting in from somewhere. I had seen, *Fire*, by Deepa Mehta. I had felt sympathy for the two women who were thrown together. I had seen Sebastien Lifshitz's *Presque Rien* and its follow up *Wild Side* only recently. I had read Oscar Wilde's *De Profundis*. I regretted the way England had treated him, despite his unusual brilliance. I had gone to see his grave in Paris. I knew of Vikram Seth's predilections. I admired his work. I firmly believed the law in India criminalizing homosexuality should be changed, just as it had been in England.

So what was wrong with me? Why was my heart beating fast with horror and indignation? Was I homophobic after all? When I was outside the gate I stopped and sat down on the dusty pavement to catch my breath. A decrepit old man in a grey beret walking by leaned over me and said, "You are very beautiful, and even if you don't go out with me, I still think so."

I gave him a look of undiluted hatred, for my heart was full of feelings I did not know I could feel, nor did I understand why I was experiencing such a strong emotion.

"I mean it," he said in a trembling voice but left when I glared at him, much to my relief.

I must have been seated there a few minutes when I saw Fabrice cross the road towards me. As soon as he was close enough I threw myself into his arms. I wept hot tears onto his good light blue shirt, and the dust from the pavement sticking to my hands soiled his neat jacket. He seemed very taken aback, but waited for me to feel more in control to ask me what the matter was.

He guided me, still shaken by occasional sobs and blinded by tears, to the café attached to the museum of the garden, and I told him what I had seen…he remembered Dodi from the evening he had spent with me and we had had tea. I didn't tell him about the hashish, though. From Fabrice, it was more important for me to know if my reaction had been in any way unjustified.

"I think you are just shocked. Not only by a sight you have never seen before in real life, but because you think it's a betrayal of trust, for this tutor to lead the half-witted pupil into activities which he may not be able to properly understand."

"Perhaps I am homophobic?" I asked him, feeling awfully primitive.

"Today there are many people who have a phobia of being homophobic," he was smiling leaning back in his chair, talking about it as if it were the most natural thing. "In the same way as many people are afraid to be racist, but let me tell you the reaction of racist people is just as strong. Once a boy I knew wanted to marry this black girl from the Ivory Coast, and his very white catholic mother had to be admitted to the hospital."

"So you are saying that I am unjustified in the way I have reacted, I am like … racist … in a way!"

"Ah, *non, cherie*," he said gently, "For you its something you haven't been exposed to."

"That's one thing we never discussed at home," I said, "although my mother would have, if she had considered it important."

"Maybe it never occurred to her."

"But Jean-François!" (I was careful not to say 'Dodi') "How does he know if he wants it? It's like Sodom and Gomorrah!"

A loud laugh broke from his lips and he brought his hand down on my arm in amusement.

"*The Bible* now!" he guffawed again, " Now look at it this way, would a poor boy like Jean-François ever find love from any other quarter? Physical love is important is it not? That is what perhaps his tutor is providing to him and which may be very good for his mental health. You wouldn't want to deprive him of the only adult love he may ever experience?"

"What if he gets AIDS? Shall I tell his mother? She goes to church."

"I wouldn't advise you to interfere in any way. This is Paris, Mehjabeen, people have a high level of tolerance towards many things that may be, at the level of the real, shocking for *you*."

"So you *are* saying I am backward."

"Ah, *non*," he said again. "You just have to learn to accept other people's realities. Maybe his mother knows. Maybe she chooses to close her eyes to it. Maybe in her youth she had had a lesbian relationship herself, so she understands it. It's quite common, you know."

I was quiet. I looked down at my fingernails. I was torn between trying to overcome my "backwardness", and the feeling that there was something wrong, not with being gay *per se,* but with the relationship between Manès Trigot and Dodi. Manès had an unusual hold over Dodi, and it was perhaps because of *this*, and it dawned on me *this was the Snail and Angel thing!* Any relationship could be beautiful or be ugly. There was seduction, which wasn't always ethical, but I said not a word to Fabrice.

He took my hand, "Let me tell you a funny story," he began. "Remember that girl to whose house we went to drink absinthe?"

"Karen?"

"Yes, it's so funny," he was very amused, and little chuckles escaped him as he talked, "she was so afraid that she was homophobic; all her friends looked down upon her and thought her really narrow minded for her views … so afraid was she, that last year she decided it was time to end this exclusion, and she got into a relationship with one of the women authors whose book she was illustrating. She began to live in with her, but after only a month they were parted, and Karen had to go into therapy. It was silly of her. One need not experience another's reality in order to understand it or accept it."

I thought my fear of being thought backward was even greater than Karen's, as I belonged to a 'conservative' country.

Anyway, we spoke no more about it, although the whole evening I was in a kind of daze, but I tried my best to appear normal, and we had dinner at the Quartier Latin, in a quiet Italian restaurant right at the back, and Fabrice held my hand and we walked up and down the river bank after dinner, looking at the books in the kiosks of the *bouquinistes* and Fabrice bought me a keychain in the shape of Pierrot in the crescent moon with 'M' inscribed in it. I wanted to get him something too, but he said my gift should come from India, and refused to let me buy anything.

I did not see Marina when I returned to Montmartre, since it was late and I went straight to bed, but I said to myself that I *would* tell at least Marina what I had witnessed. The horror of it was so great despite my conversation with Fabrice that I found myself wishing I would *never, never,* see Manès Trigot again. The thought of those pale, swivelly hands made me shudder violently in revulsion.

I couldn't trust my judgment completely, much to my chagrin. How could I be certain my instincts were right? I was only young and inexperienced and in a new land. The ground seemed to be slipping beneath my feet. I tossed and turned in my bed. Perhaps Fabrice was right. Perhaps a loving touch might help Dodi; isn't that what Doctor Pinel and then Dr. Prost of the Folie Sandrin had indirectly advocated? How could I appreciate the theory and reject its application? But was *that love*? Maybe I shouldn't be of so much *mauvaise foi* as Agnès had remonstrated that very morning.

***

It was still early the next morning when the phone rang. Fabrice said he had forgotten to tell me the night before that Monsieur Houllebecq had called him. He had invited us both to spend a few days with him at Peille; was I interested? He said we could go for three days in all, as work did not permit him to take a longer holiday at the moment. I was, naturally, thrilled at the prospect and I said yes immediately. Fabrice suggested we should leave the following weekend and return on Tuesday. We would go by train and then a friend at Saint-Raphaël would lend him his car and we could drive along the coast to Peille. It sounded too good to be true.

Life was still falling about me like a pack of cards but now I had the false impression of being part of the tableau, part of the life of Agnès Desmoulins, Dodi, and Marina. In some way I felt I was as responsible for them, as they were for my well being. They were treating me almost like family, and I had to reciprocate. But after the happenings of the previous afternoon, things seemed to have changed. I could not speak to Agnès of what I had seen. I thought I must, but my fear of my own lack of comprehension of a foreign culture stayed me. Cultures were vastly different after all. I thought I knew what was right and what was wrong, but Fabrice had showed me that we can only judge things for ourselves, not for others. About the hashish, I suppose I knew Agnès must be told if indeed it were producing an undesirable effect on Dodi. This was exactly the opposite of what I had seen in my own country. Opium was often used to quiet babies when their mothers were working in the fields. The mentally challenged were often administered such calmants in villages, in small towns, because they lived within the society, like Dodi did. They were rarely "put away". Even if they needed to be put away, there were few institutions for them. Dodi had to take some medication, I knew, a tablet every day, but I had not asked what it was. Now I found myself wondering if the effect of the hashish would in any way interfere with his medication. At the same time I knew that it was more a question of possibilities than of an immediate threat to Dodi. The danger lay in his developing an addiction. The danger lay in the blind trust he put in Monsieur Trigot, as did his mother.

Therefore I was happy at the thought of getting away with Fabrice to the Riviera for even three days. Maybe my perspective would change by the time I returned. Maybe I would find myself more detached.

I could not, under any circumstances, leave without bidding them goodbye, and so the evening I left I paid them a visit. No, luckily "the tutor" wasn't there. How ironical those words sounded to me now!

Agnès said I wasn't looking my usual self, and shouldn't I see the doctor before I left? I thanked her for her concern and said I had not slept well the night before. Marina came to the door to see me out, as Agnès was occupied with some work. She carried Mekel astride her hip and he was pulling at the clips in her hair. He had begun to say one or two words, in French, and his eyes looked much brighter than when I had first seen him. His hair too had acquired a shine. It was good to see him improving so quickly. I said so to Marina. Then I caught her by the hand and dragged her further out into the courtyard.

"Marina!" I cried, "I have seen the most awful sight! We were right about Monsieur Trigot. He is leading Dodi on in many directions." I proceeded to tell her what I had seen.

She listened incredulously, then laid a hand on my arm, "Now go with a peaceful mind, *hermana*, nothing will happen in three days. This is not so serious; I have seen worse things in the Mezquital, much worse. When you return we shall think up something. Perhaps I shall ask Lorenzo to keep an eye on them if he is free."

I felt better, and we hugged each other. Mekel pulled my hair in a parting gesture.

12
THE GIFT OF THE MEDITERRANEAN

I met Fabrice at the Gare du Nord. He had already bought the tickets to Saint-Raphaël, and we had sleeper berths. The train was to arrive at its destination early the next morning. Again Fabrice and I were together. I felt a sense of contentment, of completeness, just being in his company, and the prospect of three days with him was like a dream indeed. I would never forget them, I vowed to myself. If I had decided that I would not spend my life with this wonderful young man, it was a decision I had taken for reasons other than what I felt for him at that moment. The simple touch of his smooth cool hands on mine told me I was forgoing something I may live to regret. The transience of our companionship made it all the more precious to me. I stole a glance at Fabrice ; the TGV's speed was making my ears pop. He caught my look and smiled, an endearing smile, his green-brown eyes alight with affection. I wanted to ruffle his hair, to throw my arms around his neck and hold him tight. Yes, Dodi the Snail and his Angel were forgotten.

A car was waiting for us when we left the station at Saint-Raphaël, early the next morning. The sea air braced us out of our train-sleep, and we were driven along the coast to an old villa called *Les Saules Pleureurs* (Weeping Willows), not far from the town, built at several different levels on the coastline. This daybreak view was my first encounter with the Mediterranean. The water was like silk in the grey morning light, filled with reflections of the lightening sky—across this water Monsieur Desmoulins had sailed away from Jean-François, the Unloved, and Agnès, across this Emir had sailed towards Agnès and Dodi the Beloved; across this blue-greyness lived the Kabylies of Khadija's dreams, across this soft canopy of the morning had travelled the unknown visitors at *The Bereavement of Agnès Desmoulins.*

The hills rose emerald and pink in the intensifying sunlight to one side, and the sea darkened its azure transparence as we sat in the verandah of the villa with Jean-Marie and his wife Elisabeth. The agaves in blossom stretched their golden lamp-like necks into every scene, and the waves lapped ceaselessly on the sandy rocks. The air smelt of pine and of eucalypt, and the salty sea. We had coffee and croissants. It was so quiet, so quiet ... despite the constant whispering of the waves.

Elisabeth was a thin, silent woman, who smoked incessantly, and looked out at the sea almost like Khadija of my painting. Her eyes were an unusual luminous brown, and she spoke very little and very rapidly. But she made me feel comfortable, and I was grateful for her hospitality. Jean-Marie was younger than her perhaps by a few years, with nothing unusual about him, and he lacked the perspicacious incisiveness of most Frenchmen. He was a furniture dealer and she was writing a book on African folktales. I was dying to ask her about her book, but she was rather vague on the matter, out of the general the vagueness of her nature, and we had little time, so my curiosity remained unsatisfied. The little I gleaned was from her conversation with Fabrice, which was full of names and dates. I made a mental note to ask Fabrice about it later, very discreetly.

It was perhaps wiser to concentrate on the extraordinary beauty of the Riviera. As I looked around, I discerned the steps going down the verandah leading to a small cove and a tiny private beach, part rocky, part sandy. Jean-Marie noticed the subject of my interest, and he said if we stayed till midday we could swim in the inlet, as then the water was warm and calm. Fabrice agreed readily for we had no deadline to meet. Elisabeth would lend me a swimsuit.

I went into the ancient bathroom, where there was still no running water, and hastily razored my calves and underarms, as I had had no opportunity to swim for weeks I had neglected this aspect of my toilet altogether. The swimsuit was a deep blue, which set off my brown skin, and the tiny skirt at the hip made my legs look longer. The neckline was deep, but not being possessed of a generous bosom, it did not bother me. I regarded myself in the rusty oval mirror in the bathroom that quite flattered me. Still, I felt horribly shy and gauche as the four of us walked down to the water, but I don't think any of them noticed. Not even Fabrice, which surprised me.

The sea was so calm and clear, I caught my breath at its beauty, and because the water was still cold to me, although Jean-Marie insisted it was warm. I normally swam well, and struck out towards a rock not far from the beach. As soon as you disturbed the water, it seemed to join together once more, re-form the reflection of the sky and the wooded hills. I was reminded of the description of the Mediterranean in Shelley's "Ode to the West Wind" that had been part of my school course. Fabrice was swimming after me. I heard the splashing sound behind me, and then he reached up to me and put his arms about my waist.

"You *are* beautiful," he said, "You have a beautiful body. I want you so much."

"Thanks, Fabrice," I replied, unable to breathe.

"Thanks!"he let out an incredulous guffaw,still holding me. "You are funny, Mehjabeen! No one's ever responded to my advances like that."

I disengaged myself, for fear of losing my head, and swam away from him a little distance.

"Look Fabrice," I said, "see how the hills and clouds are reflected in the water; the summer dreams of the Mediterranean!"

"*Thou who didst waken from his summer dreams*" I quoted"*The blue Mediterranean, where he lay, Lulled by the coil of his crystalline streams,*"

Fabrice came closer, looked into my eyes and continued from the poem …

"*Beside a pumice isle in Baiae's bay, And saw in sleep old palaces and towers Quivering within the wave's intenser day.*"

I had never felt such communion with anyone. I let him come closer and I kissed him as wildly and he kissed me. I thought I would never get my breath back to swim to the beach from the rock.

The recurring thought "*What will Daddy say*?" seemed to have grown wings and flown away the moment I had entered the Mediterranean that day. Finally I could say "*Je suis.*" Conjugating the verb wasn't such an absurdity after all.

As we swam back, it occurred to me that I had so far regarded the sea in my art as a body of water that separated people and lands. The living, breathing, feeling entity that was the Mediterranean, that I acknowledged now, I had completely missed. It had a life of its own that was outside of any role it may play in the lives of the people who lived upon it. This Shelley had perceived, but I had not comprehended, even after reading his poetry. Being immersed in it had allowed me to understand better its character. I would have to work on the sea in my second painting, with Khadija and Agnès looking out onto something that wasn't just some "thing" or carrier!How would I do that now?

I avoided looking at Fabrice as we swam, so full of emotion was I, so much upheaval there was in my heart.

Back at the villa, bathed in fresh hot water, I helped Jean-Marie make omelettes stuffed with olives, while Elisabeth and Fabrice talked on the verandah. There were Italian and French cheeses, grapefruit and pineapple. There was wine, which I avoided. I ate hungrily, as a swim after a long time makes one very tired and empty and also sleepy. Jean-Marie said there was a room upstairs where I could rest for a while before we departed for the mountains. If we left at two we would be there by evening.

The room was on the level above, with large porthole style windows that looked out onto the sea and made one feel one was on board a ship. The bed, with a dusty old counterpane, was hard as rock and smelling of mould, but I would have fallen asleep almost immediately—except that Fabrice who had accompanied me upstairs, was ruffling my hair, and wishing me a restful nap.

"You will not be angry, Fabrice?" I began sleepily

"Why should I be angry, *chérie*? I am happy to be with you."

"Angry if I do not make love with you?" I said into the hard, mouldy red pillow with a design of white circles printed on it.

He looked wistful. "I will understand. I have had women since I was a boy of sixteen. But you don't know what you are missing out on!"

"Am I backward?" I said into the awful pillow once more.

He smiled, "No, I don't think so, just a bit confused."

He left the room. My longing for him seared through my body like the proverbial fire.He had been right, when he had said that one day I would long for him as he longed for me. I could hear his voice downstairs, he was talking to Jean-Marie as I drifted into slumber, for I was too tired to stay awake.

When I awoke about an hour later, there seemed to be no

one about. I tiptoed downstairs and called out softly to Elisabeth. Only Jean-Marie was there, reading the paper.He said Elisabeth and Fabrice had driven back to Saint-Raphaël for provisions we would require on the way. I sat with him and he offered me some cola. My sleep had calmed my awakened senses, but I wondered how the next two days could be spent with Fabrice without coming closer, much closer, to him.

***

As we drove up the hill in our little borrowed Renault, up the emerald and pink hill, the sea fell away farther and farther to the right, hundreds of metres. It glittered in the midday sun as though lit with a million diamonds that broke continuously upon its surface to reveal bits of cobalt blue underneath, and where the clouds prevented the sun from reaching directly, there were abrupt patches of grey-blue calmness.

We would stop at Monaco and Cannes to sightsee on our way back perhaps, but now we would drive straight up to Peillon, the "perched" village and then on to Peille, the stacked village, *village empilé.* Oaks and maritime pines, larch and quince and spruce and sycamore and olive… Fabrice knew all the trees growing on the slopes, and he pointed out each one as we drove up at a leisurely pace. There was hardly any traffic; just an occasional truck or car passed us now and then.

All of a sudden, looking towards the sea rapidly distancing itself, I understood why my mother had felt suffocated in Rahimganj—the little town where my father had grown up and where I had grown up too—it was because she knew of the *possibilities* of freedom. She knew there was a world where you could travel up a green and pink mountain and see the sea falling away blue to one side and no one would ask you why you were going where you were going.

And Fabrice was there beside me, and I could make love to him if I wanted. I was free to do as I wanted with my body. I also understood that it *was* a serious part of being emancipated. In India most women have no control over their bodies, over the number of children they will have, the age they will marry. My *Nani*, my grandmother, the poet, had partly taken away that freedom from my mother, and sent her backwards in time by marrying her off at the age of eighteen, but I, I could vindicate her losses. I must vindicate her losses. I had to cross over, to make a jump in time, before I could return.

We reached Peillon, a village sitting perched atop a rock in the most unimaginable way, and parked the car in a safe place at the entrance.

Lunch consisted of salted cod with garlic, crêpes *farçies* with shrimp and olive filling, followed by lemon tart at a medieval style restaurant. The air had become cool, there was no traffic, nor did the sound of the waves reach up so far, and I could almost hear my heart beat. We were alone, Fabrice and I. The walls of the ancient village with its stone passageways were creating intimacies of their own, with the sunlight now aslant, the flowers growing in mossy crevices—campion, thistle and devil's claw. We walked hand in hand silently, under the stone archways. Suddenly an old woman with a wooden cart rattled onto the cobbled path, there were prunes on her cart, and she smiled a toothless madwoman's smile and wagged a bearded chin, Fabrice said she had been around for years and madwoman she was. – "*Voulez-vous mes pruneaux?*", "Will you buy my prunes?", she tilted her head like a child imploring an adult. Fabrice obliged her, and she thanked us, "*Ah, merçi,mes enfants! Merçi, les amoureux*!"

She had called us lovers. Fabrice gave me a meaningful look.

We explored the village, which Fabrice had visited a number of times, and when I wondered if we should be leaving for Peille, Fabrice took my hand and said there was a small place he knew down an old path, an Inn where used to stand a church that had burnt down; the inn was called after one of the flowers that grew there, *Gelofre de l'Eglise Incendiée,* meaning dianthus of the burnt church. The grassy path absorbed even the sound of our footsteps. At the end of it was an old stone building which must have been one of the outhouses of the church, now converted into an inn. It was overhung with two huge oak trees, and behind it the cliff fell away into a deep ravine. A young man received us and said they had two rooms, if we wanted to stay there for the night.

Fabrice left me there and went back to the car for our things. It was getting dark; the shadows of the pines were intensely etched on the slopes, although the sky was still blue.

We were served a light dinner of onion soup, cardoons pickled in vinegar, and some alpine vegetables. Fabrice said we should go to bed early so that we could leave at first light the next morning else Monsieur Houllebecq would wonder what had happened to us. Fabrice kissed me at the door of my room, and said, "I will miss you tonight."

I changed into my pyjamas, and lay in the large bed, listening to the sound of the crickets and the wind whispering in the pines. I wished I had the courage to be with Fabrice at that moment. A terrible restlessness grabbed my insides, and I turned from side to side. There was a small corridor between our rooms, I could cross it and tell him I missed him too. Yes, I could....

Without rings on my fingers, or bells on my toes, without henna, without turmeric, without the songs of the *nausha,* without the small decorated boat cast upon the water, without silk or gold or betel leaves, I stepped out and, without a single rite of passage crossed the *couloir* to become a woman.

I stood at his door and said "Fabrice, I miss you too."I heard his quick intake of breath and he leapt out of his bed and took me in his arms.

It was the most beautiful and most tender night of my life, the deep velvet night at the inn of the *Gelofre* with the wind caressing the trees as Fabrice and I discovered each other;as I discovered *les délices de l'amour*. It was as though the semi-darkened room were a bubble afloat, as though it were the womb from which I was being reborn, a chrysalis from which I would emerge, free and able to fly.

***

Monsieur Houllebecq's dwelling, for so it must be called,was down an impossibly narrow street in Peille, along the ramparts of the medieval fortification and the windows overlooked the River Peillon, rushing away as though on an important errand. The old painter was himself quite a *personnage*, I realized, observing him for the first time. He had a large, well-twirled, and very black moustache, obviously dyed, as the pomaded hair on his head was more salt than pepper. His teeth were perfect, and he wore gaiters, a white shirt, and a beret. He looked like a mix between a magician and a painter. The apartment was very different from the one I occupied in Paris. In fact so different that it seemed to belong to someone else. The whitewashed walls were covered with canvases, and the rooms were Spartan, almost bare. The paintings on the walls were bizarre, or at least seemed so to me - the colours were garish, the figures childishly ill-formed, the expressions on the faces demoniacal, crazy.

In contrast to these horrible paintings there were exquisite photographs of birds and animals, butterflies and orchids of the woodlands of the Mediterranean—from the pink roselin, to the pine grosbeak,the alpine swift, swallows, rock partridges, gulls, and the amazing wall-creeper with its red and grey wings.There were also marmots, hares, and majestic ibexes and wolves, there was the two-tailed pasha butterfly, and the burnt orchid—all taken by *le mysterieux* Monsieur Houllebecq, as the lady with the green eyes had called him, and she had been right. Fabrice said he had never invited him before in all the years he had known him. It was probably because of me, he said, that he'd been invited. Yes, all the most curious people seemed to want to communicate with me, I thought distractedly.

Monsieur Houllebecq, like the old madwoman with the prunes, appeared to have guessed how Fabrice and I felt about each other. Perhaps it was quite apparent. He had put us both in the same room, which looked down a cliff, and was decorated with some of his worst paintings. There was a screaming old woman, a man with the face of a mad dog and a dog with a human face, and two women with broken teeth. I wondered if he ever became afraid of his work. I couldn't have lived with it.

As I was putting my stuff into the room, Monsieur Houllebecq came in.

"You paint too, don't you?" he asked me

"I am trying," I answered truthfully, "I am not sure if I am a painter."

"One should always be sure, my dear. In this ephemeral world, in this epoch of impatience, era of the disposable, something must change, and that change will be brought about by artists, writers, painters. See the people in my work ... they are the Disposables, *les Disponibles*, like plastic cups, crumpled foil wrappers, gaping, open mouthed, thrown, used, rejected ... their souls sucked out."

"But you don't have a single work in your Montmartre apartment!"

"Ah, my dear, the people in Paris are not yet ready. I will hold an exhibition when I feel they are, and then I will take my work there. The time will come when it will come."

Fabrice entered at that moment. Monsieur Houllebecq turned towards him, "This young man will see my *Disponibles,* and one day he will make a book on them; books are the only things that are not disposable. You may tear a book, but you can never suck out its soul."

I was oddly moved by what he said, but then I was in a state to be moved by anything.

We ate lunch on the patio of a small restaurant in another narrow street. The hill village, cut out in rock, is impossible to relate. Chronologically eccentric, lost, silent savage, unchanging, unmoving, like an ancient photograph, grey pricked in geranium windows, bubbling with folkloric springs, where people have a steady look in their eyes, akin to despair, where the sorceress sisters never leave the cavernous entrance to their abode, where the sunlight seems to pierce an eternal twilight, where a village idiot was now rattling down the narrow street an ancient cart, as we ate.

I was in a daze, but Monsieur Houllebecq cut into my reverie by asking me if I had met any of the people at the Montmartre building. I told him I knew the Desmoulins quite well by now.

"Ah, Agnès, an excellent person," he said, looking real for a change. "Had a lot of bad luck with that boy of hers, and her husband going off. It means she has to take care of the boy all her life. Doesn't take professional help, does she? Believes in solving her own problems. She's a courageous one, that. Now has taken in the Guatemalan girl and the child as well. Keeps a lookout for me, too. If ever I am ill, she sends up soup with Marina or Jean-François, and never forgets to ask how I am."

The quiet of the Maritime Alps is a palpable thing that envelops you. This is a France so unlike Paris. All the stress of that brilliant city remaining enclosed there, not filtering one bit into the alpine regions . . . yet so unlike Grenoble.

I knew the beauty of the world at that time wasn't just an external beauty. The beauty I experienced internally was reflected onto the world outside.

In the night, our dreadful companions in the paintings leered more hideously at us.

"I cannot sleep here, Fabrice," I said.

He was amused. "We can turn them around."

"They will still be there, looking at the walls."

"You *are* imaginative, *ma chère*!"

I walked out onto the small terrace, which connected our room to the living room;luckily Monsieur Houllebecq was there, and he saw me. He came out and asked me if I needed anything.

"Monsieur," I said beseechingly, "The paintings in the room are giving me insomnia!"

He was amused too, like Fabrice. "*Ça vous fait peur?*" he asked me if they frightened me. "You understand that paintings are not just figures and lines on a canvas. I appreciate that. Yes, paintings first appear, then *live* in their own way once they have been created and they affect our lives too … you understand that, I see. "

It was so dark and quiet, and the man's eyes gleamed so strangely, with a conviction I could not refute, I wanted to run. I went back quickly to the room excusing myself.

In a few moments Monsieur Houllebecq was knocking at the other door. He said he had come to take away his *Disponibles*. He took them off the wall and one by one and out of the room. I shivered as he took away the mad-dog-man. I thanked him, and he smiled enigmatically at me, as though it were something between us that Fabrice couldn't understand. It was true, too.

I felt relieved, although Fabrice said he was a bit embarrassed. I told him the artist understood, and I never told him that I was afraid of my own painting back in Paris. Surely he would think me mad.

I looked into Fabrice's green eyes as he held me in his arms. Yes, he was beautiful, and his desire for me was the most alluring thing I had ever experienced, but when I looked into his eyes I saw only Fabrice whilst when I had looked into Rahul's eyes, although he had not so much as held my hand, I saw everyone I had ever loved, everything I had ever cherished. It was too late to think of him now, he was gone. I held Fabrice against me as hard as I could, and the pain of Rahul's loss that had suddenly risen, ebbed again.

13
TROUBLE IN PARIS

Sleep has always been my enemy and my best friend. It takes me away in dreams into worlds I do not know, transforms me into people I do not recognize, and when I wake up, yesterday too becomes a dream until I step again into the present to remember who and why I am, where I am. So Sleep took from me, once I reached Paris, the intense and tender love I had felt for Fabrice, moulding it in the night with its dark, magical fingers, kneading it with unknown elements, till its colours became unrecognizable, till its shapes became two-dimensional and overlapping, and I awoke more the person I had left, than the person I had returned.

Yes, I had changed, but not that much. The Mediterranean had gifted me a love, but a love that had not become part of my soul, that did not haunt my dreams.

"Will you still go back to India?" Fabrice had asked me that night at Monsieur Houllebecq's.

"Yes, Fabrice, my life is there" I had said.

"I will come for you."

We had parted at the metro, Fabrice and I, as it was evening, and he had work the next morning. I could not thank him enough, I said. He said if I was thanking him then he too should thank me.

"You are an emancipated woman at last," he smiled as we left each other.

"No, Fabrice, make no mistake, it is because you were you," I had replied.

***

Not seeing Marina about, I went the next morning towards the Place du Tertre. Paris seemed so dry, so cold, so noisy, after Peille. I did not see Rezwan at his window. It was shut. I was surprised, as normally it was open by nine. Abdurraheim was serving tables and he nodded to me. I went up and asked why Rezwan's window was shut.

"His boys got involved in a racial clash; the police took them away for questioning, then let them go the next day. But Rezwan has not come since Saturday."

My heart stopped. Those two high-spirited adolescents, Qadir and Ahmed Messali, named after revolutionaries, who were doing so well at school ... in the police lock-up! Poor Ferhat! Poor Rezwan! I thought.

"They are good boys..." Abduraheim went on, "Someone must have provoked them badly."

"Is everything all right now?" I asked

"Yes," said Abdurraheim, wiping perspiration off his brow; he was obviously deeply troubled. "First it happened to my son, now Rezwan's boys. My boy Mohammed is rowdy, I agree, quick to anger, but Qadir and Ahmed are studious children. Never offend anybody."

The American with the guitar was sitting in front of Bernardo and Anita's easels and said he was composing a song. I told Anita about Rezwan's sons. She shrugged non-committally. She knew already, but it was of little importance to her, it seemed.

"Luckily Italy didn't colonize any country," she said, "Otherwise we would be having the same problems with immigrants."

The American suddenly looked up from his creative reverie, "Italy wasn't able to. It invaded Ethiopia in 1895. It was Ethiopia that had modern weapons and a lot of unity among the different ethnic groups, so it was able to defeat the Italian forces."

I looked at the singer for the first time. From under his scruffy hair and beard, a pair of deeply set intelligent blue eyes peered out. He saw me looking at him curiously and said "Hi!"

Then he looked at me again and disparagingly at his own dishevelled outfit, and said "Yes, I am educated. I did my masters in Modern History from Cornell. I am going back next month. I am enrolled in the PhD program."

A kind of antagonism was crackling between him and Anita, and he got up and left. I was rather sorry to see him go, for I had been expecting a new song. He stood under the awning of a café facing the Place du Tertre, and beckoned to me. He was so tall he had to bend under the awning.

When I went up to him, he smiled, "You want to hear my new song? It's called *Call in the Aliens!* It's not all done, but this is how it begins..." he picked at the strings of his guitar,

"I think we're going to need aliens,
for us to remember we're all humans,
yes, that's what we need, aliens,
an alien invasion..."

I began to laugh, and he did too.

"I know you think I'll never make a good songwriter," he said

"No, of course not!" I said, embarrassed, "I was just thinking that there will be some humans who will sell out to the aliens too!"

"Yes, I know many in my country who would do that."

"In mine, too. What's your Ph.D thesis?"

"Migrations and Ethnic Conflict in the Twentieth Century: Origins and Solutions." He held out his hand, "The name's Tim. Tim Brock."

"Mehjabeen," I said, taking his hand.

"Pleased to meet you," he responded politely, bowed and left.

I went back to Anita and Bernardo, but I didn't have the heart to talk of light things or even art, and I didn't want to talk about Rezwan, who was only a poor Berber immigrant after all, for most people. I said I was tired and returned to my room.

I did not want to paint. The Other World, the Image world, had receded in the face of the contingencies of the real world, taking with it the possibilities of optional existences. Everything appeared dull and without meaning. What trick of the mind could change or alter the fact that Rezwan's boys had been taken away by the police? The Inner World had little power over the real, no, not in the immediate plane.

I took out an encyclopedia of art from Monsieur Houllebecq's shelf, and decided to spend the day indoors.

I didn't want to see Agnès, if I couldn't tell her Dodi must be saved from Monsieur Trigot. I didn't want to call Fabrice as I didn't want to talk to him about Rezwan's boys—*les disponibles* in Paris. It was uppermost on my mind. I was sick at heart. I wished Marina would come visit me, with Malko. They were so real.

I would probably have spent the day moping, not seeing anyone, not answering calls, except my Daddy's, and perhaps I would have taken the decision to confirm a booking to New Delhi or Bombay at the earliest. Yes, that's what I would've probably done if it hadn't been for Lorenzo.

An unknown Parisian number kept calling my cell all afternoon. I didn't answer. Then at about four, there was a knocking at my door, and feeling sure it was Marina I leapt to answer it. Lorenzo stood outside, looking awkward.

I wondered who had let him into the building, but it would have been Marina of course.

"Hello," I said, and he must have read the surprise on my face.

"Do you think I could come in for a moment? I need your help."

"Of course," I said, although, in all truth, I was a little apprehensive. There was something about him ... something animal, a boldness that frightened me. But at that moment he looked anything but bold. He sat down, hunched in his chair, rested his chin on his hands and stared at his toes.

"What has happened?" I asked, feeling certain it must have something to do with Marina.

"I came to see her. She's refused to marry me."

Relief flooded through me, in spite of my sympathy for poor Lorenzo.

"Why, Lorenzo?" I asked as kindly as I could.

Then he started speaking, very fast, gesturing almost wildly in his distress: "It's because Mme Desmoulins saw us together and she asked Marina about me. Marina told her she wanted to marry me, that I would adopt Mekel, and since then the lady has stopped talking to Marina. She does not say a word to her, and Marina can't take it, you understand, she can't take it! Can't you talk to her? To Mme Desmoulins?"

"I?" I was surprised. If Marina who had lived as a daughter with Agnès for so many months, couldn't talk to her, how could I? What could I say, except that Marina needed a man's arms about her, a man's love, that she needed to hear her own tongue spoken? Was Marina to sacrifice her youth and her desires for the sake for safety and for her child? Yet isn't that what I had told Fabrice? Isn't that exactly what I had told him? That for the sake of a social position, for a husband, a home, financial security, security for her children, a woman in India would give up all her natural desires? Now wasn't that what I wanted from Marina? That she should be safe, that Malko should have a future despite her having to brave loneliness and arms empty of a man's love? I, who had experienced the beauty of lovemaking only so recently, I who had thrown caution to the winds for a primitive longing, I who had learnt only now that this also *was* freedom? Did Marina's position exclude her from the right to freedom because *she must be grateful*?

I offered Lorenzo coffee and a pizza heated in the microwave, poor man, how lost he looked. The truth was that at one level I did not want to help him. And the bitter truth was that it was partly because he was poor and not settled. That he could not be trusted. Had it been a well established Frenchman that wanted to marry Marina, I would have been delighted to offer my assistance. So I was like everyone else after all, like Monsieur Séguin I would prevent the goat from going up the mountain into the mouth of the supposed wolf even if that meant for her to never, ever, taste the fresh and fragrant mountains grasses!

I told Lorenzo I would go visit them, Agnès and Marina, and see how things stood with them. He left, despondent. I said I would call him.

***

Agnès had a migraine. She would not let Marina help her. A doctor had been called in. But when she heard I had come to visit she asked for me. Marina's eyes were swollen with crying.

"Do something, *hermana*", she begged me, "I will not marry Lorenzo, what more does she want?'

Agnès, too, looked very pale and there were pink patches under her eyes.

"*Asseyez–vous.*" She asked me to sit, then began without

preamble: "She wants to marry a penniless young man from nowhere and leave me, who have made so much of an effort to get her legalized, who have taken care of her like a mother, and she will take Malko, and that unknown will be his father! How could she think that Meyjumbee? How could she think that?"

"I think she is in love, Agnès," I said gently. "But she has said she will not marry him now."

"Has she? Will she not run off with him and take Mekel away from this home? This is Mekel's home too, now. She will take him away into the jungle, where people have no compassion, no concern. And she is young, will she be able to take care of herself and of him? And that Spanish man? Who can be sure he will not tire of her and abandon her?"

I told her these were exactly my thoughts and she looked up, a kind of relief clearing her eyes. She wasn't being unreasonable, like an autocratic parent, if I too had felt the same. But I assured her Marina would not run away leaving her behind, because that is what I firmly believed. I realized Agnès was terrified of being abandoned herself, of again being alone with Dodi, without even Emir's friendship to keep her going.

I sat with her for a quarter of an hour. We discussed Mekel's future, which she hoped would be very bright, Agnès said. Agnès and Isabelle had already deposited a sum of money in his name, for his education, and we also discussed the deep affection Marina and Agnès shared.

"I had always wanted a daughter," Agnès said, and her eyes betrayed her involvement, "She is a lovely child. If I had had one of my own flesh and blood she would not have been more affectionate to me. How can I let her go into an unknown future?"

"Talk to her, Agnès," I pleaded on Marina's behalf, "She is miserable."

"Please call her."

Within minutes Agnès was hugging Marina and Mekel both together, saying "*Mes chers enfants!*" in a broken voice.

At this moment Dodi appeared in the doorway, and seeing his mother embracing the two, he stomped his foot angrily, muttered unintelligibly in French, flung his puppet-like arms about, slapped the doorjamb, and stomped out.

His mother sighed, "He is jealous," she said wearily. Dodi thought his mother loved *les Ombres*, the Shadows, better than she loved him. Since Mekel had grown a little bigger, Dodi had started calling him *la petite ombre,* the little shadow.

I left them together, Marina still looking stricken, for she had been forced to choose one love over another, which was unfair to her. She came to the door with me. I reassured her I would think of something, and I intended to.

Back in my room, I did not have the courage to call Lorenzo. But my mind was working, options must be found. Marina could not go to the mountain, but that should not mean she should be deprived of the fresh mountain grass.

At about eight in the evening, I got a call from London. Qadeer Mamoon was back from Pakistan! A man named Edward was calling and said if I were to come, I should inform him and he would receive me at the airport, or Victoria Coach Station, or St Pancras, depending on my mode of transport. I took down his number, and began to mentally plan my trip. I would go for only a few days, and without Fabrice this time. He would prove too much of a distraction, this was something I had to do alone.

***

The next morning things were clear to me. I would go to London for a few days, and in Agnès' presence, I would entrust the keys of my apartment to Marina. It was simple enough.

I called Fabrice and told him I was going to London and I also told him I would prefer to go without him, and the reason for my decision.

Fabrice laughed, "I understand,' he said, "Earlier I would have accompanied you more to take care of you, now I would like the pleasure of your company, a selfish pleasure."

He said going to London from Paris was easy enough. You could take a late night bus and you were there early morning. Or, one could opt for a Eurostar Channel train. It cost about fifty euros return.

I could take a metro to the Gare du Nord and the Eurostar from there, but Fabrice insisted on coming to drop me. He bought my return ticket online and said he had it printed out to give me when I met him.

I was to leave the very next day. I went to say goodbye to Agnès, Marina and Malko…

"I used to travel to London often in my student days," said Agnès. "I had a friend in Oxford. We used to take the bus from Porte Maillot to Calais, then get on the P&O Ferries, cross the channel, get off at Dover, and take the bus to London. Now the bus takes only an hour or so I believe, to cross under the channel."

I handed the keys of Monsieur Houllebecq's flat to Marina while Agnès talked, and Marina understood. Her face lit up and she said she would look after the flat while I was gone. Only four or five days, I said.

I sat in the train and Fabrice sat with me, holding my hand. It was strange, I felt no desire to touch him. My entire relationship with Fabrice was strange, although for him it was natural and he had a steady attitude towards me. I was the one who vacillated in my feelings towards him. It was difficult for me to understand them; suddenly he was there like a burning desire, then I slept him off like a jet lag, and couldn't connect with anymore than I had done before Peillon. It was as if Peillon had never happened. I was elsewhere in my thoughts, and my guilt over my own unsteadiness was like a live thing in my abdomen that I was trying to get control over, but couldn't. So when Fabrice kissed me I made a great effort to genuinely kiss him back, but I saw a look of puzzlement in his eyes as we said goodbye.

14
LONDON

Edward, a quiet young man in a brown suit that matched his hair and eyes exactly received me at the St Pancras International. I was full of admiration for the station which was more like an elite shopping mall.

I saw many Indians and Pakistanis, or so I thought they were. It struck me they had a look in their eyes which was very similar to that of the North Africans in Paris, something defensive, something lost. Would Qadeer *Mamoon* be like that too? He had had a flourishing business in England, Edward told me on the way, but now he was giving away his fortune to help improve the lot of the frontier peoples of Pakistan, and the Swat Valley in particular, where his mother's ancestors belonged. He himself had grown up in Benares.

As we drove down to Qadeer *Mamoon's* home near Trafalgar Square, Edward asked me if I would like to do some sightseeing while I was there. The London Eye, Madame Tussaud's, a boat trip down the Thames, the Tower of London to see the Kohinoor diamond? "No thank you," I said, "another time." I wanted to spend time with Qadeer *Mamoon*. I saw London whizzing by, all brown and white like a huge chocolate cake with whipped cream icing through which we were driving in a minute toy car.

When we stopped in front of the semi detached stone building, and I climbed up the stone steps of the apartment holding the cold metal of the wrought iron banister, I felt I was going back into another time, again I was me, and I was Mummy and I was *Nani*. I was taking a journey into the past, my past by proxy, as though I had become connected directly from *Isfahan* in Rahimganj to this doorstep, and everything else had just been passing scenery from the window of a train. The wind blew my hair into my eyes and I bent my head against it as Edward held the door open for me.

It was quiet inside, the teakwood panelling and the Persian carpets absorbing all extraneous sounds. We were in a spacious hall, and the wide staircase led up to the rooms occupied by the old gentlemen, as he was not in a condition to move up and down on a daily basis, Edward said to me. On the right was a beautifully decorated sitting room with wickerwork furniture, chintz upholstery and damask curtains, and through the closed glass doors on the left I could see the dining room with bamboo chairs, and a glass topped table in bamboo. The windows were all mullioned and some had stained-glass details.

We went up the stairs and on the first landing there were two doors, one was a morning room and the other was a small but charming suite with a dressing room and a bathroom which had been prepared for me. He left me then, saying he would be back in fifteen minutes to take me to see my uncle. Uncle, or would he be more a granduncle? I wondered. The large windows of the bedroom looked out onto a small enclosed garden with stone landscaping and terracotta figurines. The counterpane on the bed was a light blue with a lilac floral print, and the wallpaper had trellises of wisteria and roses. There was a window seat with cushions, and a panelled alcove with a bookshelf.

The cast iron fireplace had cheeks with art-nouveau tiles, but it had obviously not been used in years. There was a picture over the fireplace, a picture I had seen before, it was my grandmother in a black dress. This was her room! Yes, this must have been her room!

In exactly fifteen minutes Edward was knocking at the door, and he led me up the carpeted stairs to see our Qadeer *Mamoon*.

My mother had described Qadeer *Mamoon* as a corpulent man with a bald head, hairy ears, a sad face, and almost female mammae. A laughable picture. But the frail man I saw sitting in his wheelchair by the window brought a lump to my throat. Edward left us, as soon as I entered.

Qadeer *Mamoon* looked at me with rheumy eyes, he was not yet eighty, but his illness had aged him prematurely.

"Come here," he said, in a deep, kindly voice. I went up to him. He took my hand and peered into my face. "Let me look at you," he said, "Mehjabeen." He spoke my name as though he had known me forever, and was rechristening me. He smiled, drew me to him and kissed my forehead. "Speak, say something, so that I may hear your voice." But the lump in my throat was so large it wouldn't let my voice through.

Seeming to understand, he pointed to a chair in front of him, "Sit there, and we will have tea first." He pressed a bell near him and a butler entered with tea on a silver tray in a silver tea service. The bone china was so light I nearly dropped the cup, and because my hand trembled so. I gulped down my tea to swallow the lump that refused to go away, but finally I could speak.

"Qadeer *Mamoon*, thank you for inviting me."

"You even have Saira's voice," he said. Saira, my grandmother, the poet, his great love.

"I was quite taken aback when I saw you. You are the spitting image of her. Perhaps your lips are a little fuller, she had a wider mouth, but your expression is very similar."

After tea he indicated a carved wooden chest by the window and asked me to open it. Inside I found two leather-bound albums, which I brought to him.

The pictures of my mother with my grandmother, quiet pictures, mostly black and white, without false smiles, had been taken by Qadeer *Mamoon*. They stared out at me from the pages of the album, and I was a bungee jumper leaping towards a past of which I was part, yet where I was not, and would never be. My grandmother was mostly in black or white. She wore saris and western dresses with equal ease it seemed. There was a picture of Lise, and some of Mummy with Zamurrad. Isaac and Tova were there too, but the sun was in their faces and one could barely discern their features. Qadeer *Mamoon* pointed them all out.

"Why did my mother not have any of these pictures?" I asked, perplexed.

"Saira did not expect to die so suddenly," Qadeer *Mamoon* sounded sad even after so many years, "Several of these were with her. She must have planned to give them to Nasreen at some point, but she did not reach that point. No one expects to die when they are young. And when you do expect it, you continue to live."

The lump was back in my throat. I would die too, I thought, die young. My mother and grandmother had both died young. It was our legacy, perhaps

"I have another thing to show you", he said. He took out something from the jacket of the album, it was a handwritten page, a poem, and there were two or three photocopies. He handed me one of the copies.

"This was an unpublished poem that had remained with me, by some chance. It is not in any of her collections."

"My grandmother's?"

"Yes. I have had a copy made for you. Keep it safely."

I made to read it, but Qadeer *Mamoon* said I must read it by myself. Perhaps he could not bear to have me read it there. I do not know.

He spoke to me then about my mother's life, and how they travelled the continent together. He said my mother had been an adorable child, and after her wedding he did not see her until the time Saira died in Paris. I told him about Zamurrad having left in a little boat down the Isère, and all he said was, "Poor little girls, they were inseparable." He believed me, I could see. When you are close to the end yourself, you cannot afford to deny the reality of others. And he had never been that kind of man anyway.

We talked until the light left the windows, and Edward said it was time for Qadeer *Mamoon* to eat his supper and take his medication. He was tired and I would be served my meal in my room.

As I left, Qadeer *Mamoon* said to me, "Mehjabeen, in your room, you will find your grandmothers clothes, take any you want, if you will wear them. But I want you to do one thing. Please put on her black woollen dress, there is only one, and tomorrow I will get a photographer to take a picture of you. You are so like her."

The night nurse arrived, a pretty young girl of Indian origin called Rekha.

***

The butler brought dinner to my room. There was *roti* and *dal* and *keema-matar*. It was a pleasant surprise to eat an Indian meal after a long time. When it was cleared away, I closed the door, and from my purse took out my *Nani's* unpublished poem, written in her clear, bold hand:

I sit and listen
To the quiet sermon of the night

And the moon emerges,
A priest clothed in a sad evanescent light
Tardy as all our thoughts
Lonely as our desires
Drooping, lopsided, pellucid,
Announced by the raucous lapwing.

Change, change, change.

It rings in the quiet air,
And hangs heavy on the moondrops
And I know its path:
That it will distance itself, and return,and leave again,
and changed, return again.

Desert, forest, river, sea, mountain, valley
Eternal image: moonrise.

I read it over and over till I knew it almost by heart. Yes, cyclical change was all there was ... and moonrise.

Then I put out the light and lay on the wide bed. The clouds and been blown away by the wind, and the waning yellow moon hung low in the window, exactly as in the poem, shedding its lightless glow against the indigo backdrop of the sky. Yes, this had been my *Nani's* room, hers this bed. There was no lapwing, but soon the wild city foxes began to wail in the night, and I had never heard a sound so terrifying. I thought of *los nahuales,* of the werepeople, and I understood why the English traditionally hunted foxes, so they would not startle them out of their beds at night!

I found it difficult to fall asleep. I was part of a past where I had not been and in the present I realized there were gaps in my existence, that at certain moments I lived in the present, then the next day it seemed they were gone and had become unlived once more.

Only the verb conjugated in the past continuous could be conjugated in the present continuous and only that Present which possesses the power of becoming a Past has a Future. No, conjugating the verb wasn't so simple at all; no wonder the French were obsessed with it. As Maniglier implies, reality becomes real because of the *way* it is articulated, therefore the reality of the green-eyed woman with the cigarette became more real than mine because she had articulated it perfectly first, and the world is a war of Realities; the one who expresses it to his advantage first, wins and gets to *create* the reality that is accepted by everyone. I awoke the next morning with the light from the window falling brightly over the counterpane. It was eight already! I jumped out of bed and started to get dressed, when the butler brought in tea and toast with marmalade and butter. I felt so happy, so cared for, so secure, as I never had done in Paris. It was like being at home. Yes, one could abandon all the loneliness of a brilliant intellectual and creative life for a small ember from the hearth of a home, which is probably the reason my grandmother, the liberated and lonely poet, had cherished the presence of Qadeer *Mamoon* in her life and why she had married my mother off at so young an age to my Daddy and the love and comfort of Isfahan!

Hesitatingly I opened my *Nani's* cupboard, there were only a few dresses, *shalwar-kameez* sets, saris, and the black woollen dress folded neatly and encased in transparent packing. I unfolded it slowly on the bed; it was a plain slim cut ankle length dress with a cowl neck, and a strand of silver embroidered hibiscus flowers running down the left side. The sleeves were narrow with a small slit at the cuff. I stood before the mirror and slipped it on. It fitted me perfectly, as though it had been tailored for me. My heart rose in a swift swoop and the lump was back in my throat. I pinned my hair back as my *Nani* had done in the photograph, and there she was, back in her mirror, the poet Saira Alvi, looking out at me. I slipped on a pair of black shoes with a small heel that I found in the shoe area of the cupboard, they too fitted me, albeit a little loosely, and I bolted out of the room, almost banging into Edward who was waiting for me on the landing. I saw the look of surprise on his face although he said nothing.

Qadeer *Mamoon*, who had breakfasted and was resting in his bed, was visibly shaken to see me.

"It is unbelievable!" he said in a voice broken at places. "You are so like her, so like her! My Saira is not gone after all!" He called me to him and kissed my forehead again. "Thank you for coming, my child. I shall die in peace now."

The digital photograph was taken in the sitting room, with me posed on a low stool as my grandmother had been. I myself was taken aback at the likeness, when the picture was shown to us in Qadeer *Mamoon's* room on his television set.

In a few hours a print had been made and framed in a frame similar to the one in which my grandmother's picture was encased, and then it was put beside hers. I felt an abrupt and deep pang for my mother Nasreen, she had fallen through the spaces, had been caught in a time warp, and she would never surface. Suddenly I wanted to return to the anonymity of Paris to get away from this lineage of which my mother was not a part.

But seeing the two pictures together told me my journey, my search, was coming to its end. Something had been completed, something indefinable, intangible, that had tormented our lives so long was now resolved.

I spent most of the day by Qadeer *Mamoon's* side, talking of my *Nani* and of Mummy as she was in her childhood, and when he took a siesta after lunch, Edward showed me the house, which was tasteful and comfortable, but obviously unlived in. Edward asked me again if I were interested in sightseeing, but I said no, another time. I had no wish whatsoever to explore London. Something inside me said it was a certainty in the future and I did not want to clutter my present with it.

Saying goodbye to Qadeer *Mamoon* wasn't easy because I knew I would never see him again. He did not have many months to go. He held me close, kissed my hands and forehead. "*Khudahafiz*," he said, "May Allah be with you." And the broad shoulders, now fallen, that had carried my mother on them, shook with a dry sob. I could not speak, the lump in my throat had become so large and painful. The *Khudahafiz* I said was strangled by my tears.

Edward accompanied me to the train station, and again we cut through the chocolate cake of London. Before we parted, Edward said, "We shall meet again Miss. He is calling his lawyer to change his will. The house and everything in it is to be yours."

15
Last Tango

When I was back in Monsieur Houllebecq's apartment in Montmartre, (having taken the keys from Marina, but not having had the time to chat with her), I felt a great sense of relief to hear French, a tongue alien to me compared to English, and to be away from that past which had never let my mother go. From the image of my *Nani*, which was *me*. In Paris I could say, *je suis.* I am. And be just me, and no one else. No, I did not want to be *Nani*.

The unknowable in us is free, to connect to diverse realities, and hates to be caught in the logic of determinism. Life must go forward, Marina had said, and only forward. To me Marina's friendship was immensely valuable as was Agnès'. I knew that anything I couldn't sleep off was real to me.

And this time, returning to Paris, which was so unnecessarily cold and dark although the summer was still young, I could feel the "charge" that Graeth spoke about. I awoke the morning after my return not with a feeling of sadness for Qadeer *Mamoon*, not with longing to see Fabrice, but with a grating anxiety that had nothing to do with my own life. I felt lonely for my home, for India, for

Isfahan, for Daddy. I had not told Daddy that Qadeer *Mamoon* was willing his London home in my name. I was not excited about it, oddly enough. It was the logical culmination to a journey undertaken over three generations, that was all. But I would call him today and tell him, I promised myself.

I was, however, keen to see Marina, Agnès and Malko. As I was eating my breakfast and staring at "*The Bereavement...*" for I had not worked on the diptych for a long time now, since Peille in fact, there was a knock at my door.

It was Dodi, and he actually gave me a small smile. I thought I had never seen him smile like that.

"Would you like to come in?" I asked, always a little apprehensive in his company.

"Can I see them again?" he asked

I let him in. "Yes," I said. " In fact I was just working on the painting."

Dodi went ahead of me into the *salon*, and this time his attention was on the second painting, that of Khadija and Agnès. From time to time he bent over it and peered closely at Khadija. I sat and sipped the remaining coffee in my mug.

"See," he said presently, pointing to the figure of Khadija, "I knew there would be more of them. They are coming in hordes, and someone has got to stop them."

"Who will stop them?" I asked, for want of anything better to say. I did not expect him to have an answer.

"The Snail and the Angel, of course," he replied promptly. "They will come out of the museum and at the Espace Montmartre ... they will travel, and find them one by one."

I was quite aghast. What did this madman mean?

"Do you mean you and Manès Trigot?" I asked

"There are many snails and many angels," he said mysteriously,

"Dali made many and there are the reproductions, as in our house. They will travel."

I wanted him to leave, to go with his crazy thoughts wherever he wanted. There was something ominous in what he said, but it was not intelligible. The whole thing was taking on the colour of a horror film.

He sat down on a chair then, and asked for coffee. I made him some, thinking all the while I must speak to Agnès about everything I knew, about the hashish, about what I had seen at the Luxembourg garden. I had been distracted by my involvement with Fabrice and my visit to London. Besides I hesitated, in case Agnès did not believe me and in case all this mattered little to her, as Fabrice had suggested, as long as Manès Trigot was taking some care of Dodi who really had no one. Dodi was frowning and drinking his coffee with puppet-like movements. He was more mechanical when he was excited I had noticed. I was wishing that he would leave. But he sat there, relaxed, showing no sign of leaving. After about a quarter of an hour, during which I sat there too, not daring to go about my work, afraid he might damage my painting, he rose, saying to me, "But you forgot to put the flames."

"What flames?" I asked apprehensively.

"Under them," he said simply, and refused to speak further. He just got a very preoccupied look on his face, and left, shuffling as was his wont. I was relieved to see him go and did not want to detain him longer by conversing with him. In any case the conversation seemed quite absurd. But somewhere I felt there was always a sense to what Dodi said, although he spoke in apparent riddles.I stood at my door watching him go down. When he reached the landing he looked up unexpectedly, for he always took the stairs with great concentration, and said "Put the flames there, *d'accord?*"

He looked at the steps again not waiting for my answer, and I shut the door, not feeling good.

I went back to painting, for I had to work on the sea, and give it a life filled with *summer dreams.* I also needed to add another figure in the foreground of the painting, in the shadow, unlit by the window. The figure was a woman in a flowing dress, her head covered, a woman with a dark face and dark brows, and she was turning around and looking over her shoulder back into the room, apprehensively. One hand was at the edge of the painting, which added to the movement of her turning back … gave it a sense of timing. Why was she there? She had not come to the *Bereavement,* but she was there now, and she was afraid.

Each time I worked on the diptych I felt uneasy afterwards. I was not pleased that it was connected in some way to Dodi and his prophesies. It was afternoon by the time I finished placing the new figure, and I was hungry, and decided to go out for lunch, as I hadn't stocked the refrigerator since my visit to London. Just as I was leaving, Fabrice called.

"Fabrice," I said, "I want to book my ticket back to New Delhi." I had not thought about it, but it came out the moment I heard Fabrice's voice.

Fabrice was not happy, of course. "Why, *cherie?*" he asked, "Why all of a sudden?"

"I miss my Daddy," I wanted to say stupidly, but Fabrice would have thought me foolish, so I said, "I think I am about to complete my painting. I have also been to London. So my work here is over."

"*Et nous*?" I sensed some accusation in his voice, "What about us?" But before I could answer he said we must meet to discuss this. So we fixed a rendezvous at the Pont des Arts for the evening, and we'd go out for dinner afterwards.

I met Anita and Bernardo at the Place du Tertre but Rezwan was nowhere to be seen, and Abdurraheim told me, between waiting tables, that Rezwan's boys had gone back to school, and all was well.

Anita said the weather had really turned lousy this year and they were barely making enough to keep them in Paris now so they had decided they would go back to Padua in Italy where they belonged.

"When will you go?" I asked, saddened at their decision.

"Perhaps next week," Anita said. "But we must not loose touch. If you come back to Paris next year we will meet."

"Won't you come to India?"

"It's too expensive, and it's too vast a country. If Bernardo decides to do some good work and it sells, maybe we will go to India. But Bernardo is much too lazy for a talented man." She looked at him in mock anger. "If I had half his talent, I would be rich by now."

Bernardo screwed up his eyes and looked enigmatically at her. "I like to live," he said, "Day after day. I cannot go chasing dreams that may remain only dreams." He closed his eyes and leaned back in his small chair. The light heightened the effect of grey in his whiskers and his eyebrows, become prominent because his expressive eyes were shut.

***

After lunch I returned to my rooms, and I did not see or hear from Marina or Agnès. Their doors remained shut, there seemed to be no activity inside. Dodi too had disappeared, for which I was grateful. I will call tomorrow, I said to myself. I was slowly gearing myself up to tell Agnès everything. I was planning to leave Paris soon, anyway.

I slept a bit in the afternoon and by four was ready to leave for the Pont des Arts.

Fabrice held me very tenderly and in his arms I felt hope and my breath returning to me, and my heart beat more evenly afterwards. It was true that he had a very calming effect on me.

I told him about the house in London; that it was going to be mine. I thought it was something that would make sense to him. And it did, he said that meant I would return to Europe, even if I left now for India. We bought crêpes from a shop and sat down on the bridge, along with the dozens of students lounging there. The wind was cold and I wrapped my scarf about my ears.

"What will happen to us if you leave now?" I knew the question was coming.

"I have no answer, Fabrice," I said.

"Have you thought of me?"

"I have thought that you, who have had women since you were sixteen, will forget me and marry Jeannine who is more your kind. It would be more practical."

He looked angry. "One moment you are a little girl, too young for your years, and the next you become a grandmother and start telling me what's good for me. How do you know what is good for me or what I want?"

"Fabrice, if you have been to bed with so many women, what does one more matter?"

"It's not the going to bed, you silly girl … it's not the important thing … "

I looked at him and said slowly, "It meant a great deal to me. Because, as you said, I was not emancipated."

He was upset, very upset. "No, it didn't, and you know it. It meant a great deal to you as part of your *own* development, but it didn't have much to do with *me*!"

"No, Fabrice, no, it wouldn't have been anyone else!" I cried, appalled now at my own callousness. "It's just that I miss my home, I want to go back. I don't want to get too involved with you. And I don't want to keep you hanging on. You must get on with your life!"

"Life is not over. India isn't on the moon!" he said, "You talk as if it were!"

He got up and pulled me up firmly by the arm. "We'll see about things," he said resolutely, "You go back to India if you wish now, but don't tell me what to do with my life. You don't know what's in the future. I will decide that for us. You wait and see. I am not accepting your decision."

I was strangely reassured by his determination, and the evening passed quite pleasantly, and we did not speak again of parting.

But the next morning Fabrice's travel agent called me and asked me when I wanted to leave for India.

I hadn't yet made up my mind about the date of departure, I would have to discuss it with Daddy, but I gave the agent a tentative date two weeks from the day. Soon after, I received a call from Agnès. She never called me, so I was surprised and a little worried. I hoped everything was well with them. Agnès asked me to come over whenever it was convenient for me.

The moment I had finished breakfast I locked my door and went down. Agnès was in the front salon, on the sofa, sorting out a variety of coloured buttons. She looked composed and cheerful. Seeing her relieved my anxiety and I smiled as she kissed my cheeks. It was good to be with her again. I asked after Marina. Agnès said she had taken Malko to the clinic for his hepatitis shot. She would be back in an hour or so.

Agnès motioned for me to sit in the armchair next to her. She seemed excited about something.

"Meyjumbee," she said, almost in a whisper, bending towards me, "I have to ask for your advice on a very important matter."

It must be about Marina, I hazarded a guess, it seemed she wants to talk to me alone.

"You see," she began, almost hesitantly, "I want to get Marina married ..."

I dared not breathe ... to Lorenzo? Was it possible? Had Agnès rethought her decision after all?

"Married? I said, "To whom?"

"To Dodi. He turned twenty-one last week."

My heart plummeted in a swift plunge and I seemed to be falling down an endless abyss spinning clockwise and anticlockwise at the same time. How could Agnès have thought of this? Was I dreaming? Was this some cruel joke? Agnès, the kind, gentle Agnès!

When I could speak I asked, "Does she know?"

"I have hinted to her, and she did not seem averse to the idea. I want you to ask her and get a final answer."

I could no longer contain my resentment, "But what will her life be, Agnès, married to Dodi?"

"I knew you would ask, Meyjumbee, you are a sincere girl and you love Marina like a sister. I appreciate your asking."

There was a long silence. Agnès sighed from time to time, and continued sorting her coloured buttons.

Many thoughts chased each other around my head. I saw the sunlight reflected off the glass of the opposite flat make patterns on the carpet. Then disappear altogether as clouds obscured the sun. We are all driven by some force towards something in particular, I thought—like Madame Desmoulins, driven by the future of her son, his well-being, his acceptance, at some level, in the world in which he lived, his being adjusted to it, all mattered more to her than Marina and her child after all. Marina's sorrows must have moved her only up to a point; she did not feel responsible for them. A large part of being moved by something is a feeling of responsibility and identification. It was true it was none of her fault that Guatemala was in such a state, the people would not, in several generations overcome the psychological scars left by the civil war. Madame Desmoulins' initial interaction with Marina had not been based on selfish motives, but as time went by she must have realized the advantages of an alliance between the young woman and her mentally challenged son. I had heard of such stories in Rahimganj, where normal, healthy but destitute young women of poor families were married off to the sons of rich families who were challenged physically or mentally, often impotent young men in the hope of providing care and love for the men, sacrificing the happiness of the poor young women. The same seemed to be happening here.

Madame Desmoulins spoke at last, "You see, Monsieur Desmoulins called, he says he misses me and regrets having abandoned me. Imagine! After twenty years! He says I don't have to accept him back, but that he is building a little villa for me by the sea near his own, that he feels responsible for me and that I can go there and live with them, in my own cottage of course," she broke off and sighed again. "I am tired, Meyjumbee, so tired. I need someone to take care of me. Monsieur Desmoulins was a good husband until Dodi was born. He still does not want Dodi."

I felt sad, very sad, for her and for Marina. And for Dodi, though what he did not know wouldn't hurt him.

"But Dodi hates Marina, Agnès!" I interrupted her. This had occurred to me all of a sudden, and a ray of hope shone bright in my dark despair for Marina, only to be extinguished by Agnès' answer.

"Ah, *non, non*, he is only jealous of her. Of late he has started liking her much better; I even see him go up to her and talk these days."

I was silent again. There seemed to be nothing for me to say. Agnès had made up her mind. Only Marina had to agree.

I was watching the patterns of light on the carpet. When I looked up I saw Agnès regarding me quizzically. "You don't hate me, do you Meyjumbee?"

"No," I said truthfully, "But I am sad. I can't think of any solution."

"Time will find its own solution," she said enigmatically.

I sat there thinking. Does everything happen as if by hazard? Or are we all structured into some kind of a pattern, and like the pieces on a chess board can we only move in certain directions, only a certain number of spaces, depending upon our function and our programming?

"Will you talk to her?" Mme Desmoulins' tone was pleading.

"I will try," I said half-heartedly. How could I tell Marina she should tie herself forever to an *aliéné*? Marina, who called me her sister? How could I betray her thus?

Agnès' phone rang—Marina was calling to say there was a lengthy queue at the clinic she would take longer than expected. I was disappointed, eager to meet Marina and talk to her first, to ask her if she had used my key and if she had met Lorenzo at the apartment. I wanted to ask this before I could put Agnès' proposal to her.

Immediately after, Fabrice's travel agent called me to say they needed my passport, visa details and some signatures; could I go over to their office on the Avenue des Champs Elysées in the Sixteenth? I excused myself to Agnès, as Marina wasn't coming back in the next hour, and told her I needed to go to the travel agent.

"*Vous partez déjà*?" Agnès wanted to know if I was leaving already. I said I was booking my ticket, a tentative date, that was all. Until Marina's fate was resolved, how could I leave? I said to myself.

"All of us need to leave sometime," she said philosophically, leaning back in her seat and looking at one of the buttons in the light to see if it had flaws. I knew she was thinking of herself. But she was also thinking of imprisoning Marina or maybe Marina had already travelled a long way … had reached Paris, and would stay on.

I returned late in the evening, warmed myself some soup from a can and ate it with bread. My appetite had gone. Replaced by that grating anxiety, partly for Marina, partly for unidentifiable reasons.

It must have been past midnight when I heard a banging at my door. I groggily got out of bed and peered out. Dodi was outside my door looking angry. I shut it quickly, although he was trying to push it open.

"You didn't do it!" he shouted, "If you had put the flames when I asked you, I would have succeeded! The Snail and the Angel would have won!"

I went to the phone, trembling, and called Agnès. "Please, Dodi is at my door, banging and shouting!"

Despite the chill I went to the windows and stepped out onto the balcony. The noise had woken several of the neighbours and a few people came out onto their balconies. Others were probably familiar with Dodi's moods and continued to sleep in peace. Moments later Marina and Agnès were climbing up the stairs on my side of the building and I could hear their voices trying to calm Dodi.

"Will you come down, Meyjumbee," Agnès called out to me, "He wants to talk to you. He won't get violent, I promise."

Trusting Agnès' judgement I put on my gown and went down to their apartment, where, by now, Dodi had been ensconced in a chair, a blanket covering his knees and a mug of hot soup in his hand. He turned his face from me when I entered the room. He looked like he had been crying.

Agnès said he had just come in from Aubervilliers, he was saying it was all my fault. I hadn't painted the flames so his project had been unsuccessful. He had come alone. Manès hadn't accompanied him. It was all so strange.

Dodi wanted to talk to me alone. He said Marina and his mother must leave the room. Agnès was uneasy but he promised he would keep sitting on his chair. He was behaving unexpectedly well, I thought. But the moment Agnès and Marina left the room, (they went into the kitchen, to make some coffee they said), Dodi rose from his chair—I backed rapidly towards the door, thinking he might attack me, but he went to the chest of drawers behind the sofa and from the top drawer pulled out some newspaper cuttings. He brought them over to me.

They were about a fire that had taken place at the Paris-Opéra hotel in the IX Arrondissement of Paris, in April that year, and 24 Africans had been killed. "*Voila*," he said angrily, looking at me accusingly "*Voila, le feu*!" He never did speak very long sentences and "Here's the fire" was all he said to me. Then he put the cuttings in his pocket, turned abruptly and walked towards the door leading to the stairs. He stopped at the door and a great ugly sob escaped him. "He called me Dodi," he wept loudly, "*C'est fini! C'est fini!* He won't ever come back! The Angel is gone forever! *Je suis un râté!* I am a failure!" He climbed up the stairs, still sobbing.

I went seeking Marina and Agnès in the kitchen. I told them Dodi had shown me a newspaper cutting and then gone up to his room, sobbing. Agnès sighed and we all sat at her table and had coffee. No one spoke. That Dodi was not all there, we knew, but why had he come in so late? Why had Manès Trigot left him to travel by himself such a long distance from Aubervilliers? She tried ringing Manès on his cell, but a recorded message said, "*Ce numéro n'est pas valide*" The number did not exist.

"Maybe he has changed his number," Agnès said, puzzled. "I haven't called him in a long time. I don't know if I have called him ever. It was always he who called."

Agnès accompanied me to the other side of the courtyard, kissed me on both cheeks and apologized for Dodi's behaviour. I still did not have the heart to tell her what I knew.

It rained that night, and then the weather began to clear. Finally the summer that had evaded Paris seemed to be returning; Bernardo and Anita may not leave now, I thought, as the sunshine from the window crept onto the floor of my apartment. I was bleary eyed after the sleepless night, and it was only in the afternoon that I could leave the apartment. I would go eat a sandwich from Rezwan's window, if he wasn't too busy, I said to myself. When I arrived at the Place du Tertre, I saw Rezwan shutting down.

"Are you going already?" I asked, disappointed. Rezwan said he was leaving for the day. His brother had a problem.

"I have many things on my mind," he said with a worried smile. "You see, Khadija is *very* upset, she wants to go back to her people. You remember my sister-in-law, don't you?"

"Of course," I said. (How could I have forgotten her? She was in my painting.)"She says she wants to go back to the Kabylie Mountains. She can't stand being here in Paris any longer. We are only part Imazighen, you see, but she is wholly Amazigh. She wants to go to her family, to speak Tamazight, which we no longer speak among ourselves, we only speak Arabic, and the children only speak French. She has not been able to adjust, and … and … she has threatened to kill herself if we do not let her go," he told me all this in one big rush, as he shut down his window and locked it.

I was at a loss for words. Yes, Khadija had to leave, I had seen that, but that it should happen so soon …

I decided to walk towards the metro station with Rezwan.

"You see we'd known for sometime now that she was unhappy here. She put on a lot of weight, fought with my brother, couldn't sleep properly. We took her to a doctor, and he said the only way was that she should either find a reasonable employment or return to Algeria. But where to find employment for her?"

"Then yesterday with a strange incident happening in our building, she became paranoid and wants now to leave as soon as possible."

"What incident?" I asked

"Oh, we had a very lucky escape. At about eleven p.m. someone tried to set our building on fire."

I gasped and clutched his arm; something seemed to be fitting in. I listened intently as he spoke. We had both stopped walking and stood face to face.

"It was in the stairwell. There was an engagement party on the first floor, and there was a general commotion of guests coming and going, and suddenly there was the smell of petrol, and flames were streaking across the floor towards the banister, luckily there were many young men present and they put the fire out with blankets before it got out of hand." I was staring at him, unable to speak or move. It was all becoming clear to me.

Rezwan screwed up his eyes in an already vexed countenance and said, "I could have sworn I saw that young man, who had come with you to ask for my address one day. Just as I was coming out of the lift when I heard the uproar, but it was someone in a black monkey cap, so I couldn't really tell … what was that young man's name, the one who came with you?"

"Oh," I said, lightly, "Jean-François? That was Jean-François Desmoulins. Madame Desmoulins' son. A little off. He keeps asking people for their addresses. Asked me for mine in India, too." I lied glibly.

"No, no, couldn't have been him," Rezwan said, with a concentrated look, "This one was probably of Arab descent, there was another man with him, a thin little man, and he was calling him 'Dodi', very loudly, '*Allons, Dodi, allons-y*!' And he was steering him out of the building saying he was sick and needed to be taken to the hospital."

Some large wild rabbit seemed to have entered my chest and was clamouring to be let out. My breath had left my lungs altogether. Manès Trigot and Dodi! The Snail and the Angel!

"We didn't call the police as it may have been an accident, or maybe it was one of our own rowdy boys who thought he was playing a prank."

"I hope things work out for Khadija. Give my regards to your family", I said to Rezwan, and excusing myself as best as I could in my state of consternation, I rushed back up the hill.

I found Agnès in her kitchen cooking quenelles in a mushroom sauce. The odour of the food made me realize I hadn't eaten a thing since the morning. I was trembling violently, although it was a warm day, and Agnès made me sit down and drink a glass of grapefruit juice before she let me say anything.

I told her all. About the hashish, about the scene I witnessed at the Luxembourg garden, and now what my conversation with Rezwan had revealed. When I had finished she was trembling more than I and she burst into tears. I had never seen her so emotional before.

"And I trusted that bastard!" she cried, "How could I have been so foolish!"

Marina, hearing our voices, came down with Mekel, feeding him from a bottle. He was half asleep.

"*Que pasa*?" What is it? She cried in alarm, seeing Agnès' face.

We told her as best as we could …

Agnès phoned her sister Isabelle. She would come the next morning with Monsieur Morin, the counsellor. But it was decided between us we would keep the story of the fire to ourselves, Agnès, Marina, Isabelle and I.

Agnès suddenly brightened. She had been used to dealing with hardships all by herself; and she was strong, I supposed. She told Marina and me to go down to Montparnasse and do some window shopping and eat at a restaurant somewhere. When we said we did not want to leave her, she insisted. She said she would be okay and she would look after Mekel too, in case he awoke before we returned.

We did not go to Montparnasse. We did not do any window shopping. We walked down the Rue des Martyrs towards the Opera, and stopped at bakeries and *fromageries* and fruit shops to eat as we pleased. The sun was out and Paris looked more enticing than ever. When I thought I would soon be leaving it, I experienced a twinge of regret I could barely explain.

I took the opportunity to discuss Marina's future with her. Perhaps that is what Agnès had intended, when she sent us off together. In spite of the recent developments, I felt Agnès was still planning for Dodi and Marina; she had not been deterred from her resolve.

"Marina, Agnès told me that she has spoken to you."

Marina was quick to catch on. She had been waiting for this time alone with me too, so that she could speak to me about Agnès' proposal.

We were eating cherries out of a brown paper packet, and we sat down in one of the squares on a stone bench and looked at each other.

"When you were away in London, *hermana*," Marina began slowly, "I went to your apartment and Lorenzo came there to meet me. But when he left I think Agnès saw him going, from the upstairs window. She knows, but she doesn't speak of it. I think she feels I may leave her if she pressurizes me to leave Lorenzo."

"Are you happy?"

"I am very happy. But I don't like having to hide. Now you have returned. We will have to find another place to meet."

"Why? I am here another two weeks or so. You should have told me earlier. I could always go out for a bit."

She smiled, but her eyes were conveying something else.

"Agnès said you haven't said 'no' to marrying Dodi," I ventured

"*Hermana*", Marina said very steadily, "You know what my life has been. I am today in love with Lorenzo. Yes, I want to start a new life with him. But if, like my many fathers stopped loving my mother, if he stops loving me, then I would be at his mercy."

"And Dodi?" I was puzzled.

"Dodi will never love me. And he will never abandon me. *Mira*, with Dodi, I can be free".

"Free?"

"Yes, *hermana*, I will do as I please. He will not interfere; he will not try and rule my life. A man who can have children, *hermana* is a *male*, but not necessarily a father, or a husband. I have thought over all this. Weren't the men who raped me males? I have Mekel to show that they were, but were they human? Were they men? Who knows? Being able to reproduce is no criterion for being a man who can be married to a woman."

"You won't be lonely being married to Dodi?"

"There is Lorenzo … "

"But will he still be with you if you are Madame Jean-François Desmoulins?"

"If he leaves, well, that means he did not really love me." Marina shrugged in a sort of resigned way. "Like my fathers never loved my mother." She had indeed thought it over very carefully.

"And the responsibility of Dodi?"

"Oh, that isn't a problem. I have been helping look after him now many months; he is uncontrollable only *sometimes*. If one speaks kindly to him and does not contradict him when he is in one of his 'moods' then he calms down. There is always Isabelle to help me."

"You are very brave, Marina," I said, in awe. How much courage it would require!

"It will be like a job," Marina said, "the compensation being a home, social stability, an income, education for Mekel, and best of all, freedom from the dictates of a man."

I felt more cheerful all of a sudden. "And," Marina said , "It's the least I can do to repay Agnès for all her kindnesses to me, for giving me and my Malko a new life."

I understood. She was taking the right decision in her circumstances. And she would be liberating Agnès Desmoulins of the terrible burden of Dodi, more a burden because Agnès loved him, and therefore suffered each day. Agnès would be free, to travel across the Mediterranean, as she desired.

***

I went back to my second painting that night. The woman turning back, the woman who would not travel, the one who was afraid …what did she see? I sat awhile looking at it, touching it up … then I knew … and I began to put in, at the inner edge of the tableau, flames … red, white, orange, with blue hearts, jumping, leaping, towards the third and nameless woman. The flames reflecting off her face, gave it a more terrifying aspect, almost like the *Disponibles* of Monsieur Houllebecq's paintings. Dodi was right. Something terrible was about to happen.

***

The next morning Marina called me to say I should be at their place by eleven, as Isabelle and the counsellor were coming too. Then Fabrice called saying I had again become a stranger. I told him I was a bit busy that day, and he asked how busy could I be, and what did I have to do that was more important than meeting him over lunch? I said I had to meet some friends, that I had promised them earlier, so if he could please excuse me.

"You have become Parisian," he said ironically, "One has to take an appointment with you."

I reached Agnès' exactly at eleven, but Isabelle and Monsieur

Morin were not there yet. So I thought there was time enough to tell Agnès what Marina had decided. I found her in the kitchen as usual, making *tarte aux pommes*, and pâté sandwiches. High tea was being arranged for the visitors.

"Agnès," I said, "I have good news for you. *De bonnes nouvelles.*"

"Good news at such a time, I would indeed be grateful." her face lit up just a shade.

"Marina will marry Dodi."

Agnès stopped her work, and looked at me, "Are you sure?"

"Yes, she told me, she had thought over it and she is prepared to take on his responsibility. She says she owes it to you after all that you have done for her."

"I am willing to do more … I will not let her be unhappy, I love her like my own. Meyjumbee, you may have thought me selfish and mean, but you know each circumstance has its own solution. A unique one. I will explain to you after we have solved Dodi's present dilemma." She looked so earnest that I immediately believed her.

Isabelle rushed in like a summer squall, scolding her sister roundly for her foolishness in having trusted Manès Trigot. "*Comment t'as pu faire ça*!" she raged. Trusted the man without even knowing his phone number! Agnès said Dodi had met him at the supermarket, and he was feeling unwell, so Dodi had brought him home saying his mother would help him, then he had offered to help Dodi with his math and extended many little services to the family like mending the leaking roof and sorting out the file of electricity bills—men's jobs—in a household where there were no real men.

"How could you have let him into the house like this, knowing nothing about him?" Isabelle was still in shock.

"*Maman* would have done, he was ill." She looked like a child, I thought.

"Maman lived in different times, Agnès! Maman used to take in dogs and cats and chickens and crows! The world is not the same now." She turned to me, took me by the arm and we went into the salon.

"France has a lot of problems. Financially. There is a lot of unemployment. There is restlessness among the second generation immigrants. Because of globalization many people have lost their jobs."

"Yes," I said, "It's the same in India."

"There is resentment among the white youth too. The Right is gaining more legitimacy, drawing more people. We are afraid for France. There are those who refuse to see the dangers. We have to battle with them too."

Monsieur Morin had gone up with Dodi. He had been told that Dodi had been led astray by the tutor who had wanted to drug him and perhaps exploit him sexually. He hadn't been told about the fire, which Isabelle thought unnecessary unless Dodi himself came out with it. Then they would try and minimize its importance. She said she wasn't sure about Monsieur Morin's political leanings. One had to be very careful these days, she said, especially as her husband's position was a sensitive one.

Marina was with Mme Desmoulins, helping her. Isabelle lowered her voice to a whisper, and leaned towards me, "I know about Marina too. I guess she will never agree to Agnès' proposal. It is foolish of my sister to harbour such dreams."

I informed her that Marina had already agreed. Isabelle's face coloured, with incredulity, with relief, with uncertainty.

"Just as my husband is having the identity of this Manès Trigot investigated, we haven't found a person of such a name yet, we are also looking into the background of Lorenzo, Marina's beau. Till now he seems quite genuine. He has an old mother back in Murcia whom he must support, he has a brother in the States, a dentist, and they have a large house between them in Murcia. The brother was educated, and then their father expired. Lorenzo couldn't get an education. That's why he does these odd jobs."

I was amazed at Isabelle's farsightedness; she had thought of everything, and to what end?

"Monsieur Desmoulins, my brother in law, Agnès husband, and Dodi's father, says he will pay Lorenzo a handsome salary to be caretaker of this place and helping hand to Marina."

I thought it was all wonderful! If only Lorenzo would agree …

***

Monsieur Desmoulins looked like a sofa that had taken on human form. He came alone for the wedding, though he didn't look exactly pleased to see Dodi. Dodi was Jean-François now, of course. No one was allowed to call him Dodi, after the incident at Aubervilliers.

The weather was just gorgeous. Marina looked beautiful in white lace and a veil decorated with ornamental coloured buttons, and Dodi, properly shaven, looked smart and really happy, and he kept hugging Marina and slobbering a bit over her cheeks at the Saint-Jean Church where they were married. Lorenzo was best man and I was maid of honour, and Madame Desmoulins carried Malko, and she beamed and beamed. Isabelle was there and her terrible snobs of children, who never spoke to anyone. Isabelle's husband gave Marina away. And Monsieur Morin was there with his wife and two daughters.

I had a guest too. Fabrice. He was surprised indeed to see my closeness to the Desmoulins family, to Marina.

"You never told me you knew so many people!" he said.

"I am emancipated in many ways, dear Fabrice," I laughed.

An assortment of other people I had never met had been invited for the wedding lunch held in the courtyard. I had a great time; everything seemed to have sorted itself out in its own unique way just as Agnès had said. The following month Agnès would leave for Skikda with her husband. Across the Mediterranean.

I took Fabrice up to my rooms. I was to leave the following week, on the twenty fourth of August. He held me close, "Must you go?"

I said nothing. I would miss him too. I said I would leave my paintings with him, could he please keep them safely until I came for them? He looked cheered at that.

I took him to the salon and uncovered my diptych which was almost complete. I told him it was called "*The Bereavement of Agnès Desmoulins*". I think he was rather impressed with it. I said the only thing I couldn't really understand were the flames, if they had a meaning at all. He said he would arrange to have it collected and suitably framed before I left.

And a van arrived a few days later, and I loaded into it the diptych that had reached its end, the flames still unexplained, and I had not the time now to ponder over them. The small actions needed before departures were demanding attention: the stitching together of days and nights, of thoughts of feelings, putting them all in their proper little bags and sewing them up, the seeing of them in perspective, the allocation of kisses and tears, the dividing of love and promises of return; in the midst of it all I saw for the last time the pied eyes of the Piper, one blue one green, looking meaningfully out at me from the canvas, and I was no longer afraid, because I had done what I could. And I saw the van disappearing down the winding Montmartre street, and when it had gone, the Other World came in to sit about a while as I set the apartment in order and wrote a thank you note to the owner, wishing him the best for his pending exhibition of *Les Disponibles* in Paris, and as I locked the door for the last time, the Image World, the world of Nerval and Dali, too, seemed to recede into the shadows of Montmartre, down the Rue des Norvins, down the Allée des Brouillards, the Street of Mists, and I wondered if I could still pass through the little door inside me and perceive an alternate reality, or, would it just swoosh past me and I would lose it in the air thousands of miles above the earth on the plane to India!

16
Lives as They Should Be

Ammi Dadi sent Qamrun to the lawn where I sat in the February sunshine. There were dates and cashew nuts in a silver bowl. Alongside was a silver glass of almond milk with saffron. My life was of an astonishing beauty.

Daddy was in the office, his new air-conditioned office in Sabz Gali. He had printed out my emails of the week, and sent them with his peon, and I could read them at leisure in the sun. There was still no Internet at Isfahan.

It was cold in the shade, and inside. *Ouqouqouq,* a bird said occasionally from the orchard. My aunt, Zehra *Phuphi* was singing strains from an old Hindi film melody, her high sweet voice, sometimes off-key, alternating with the deep notes of the hidden bird.

Qadeer Mamoon had passed away in December. Edward mailed saying I would have to either appoint a lawyer, or, go over myself to sign all the necessary documents for the house. He was in charge of it in the meantime.

Fabrice wanted me to come back to Paris. He wasn't marrying Jeannine. He was offering me three books to illustrate (not marriage).

I would think about it after I finished my graphic design course. He loved the diptych more every day, he said. He had it hanging in his living space.

I had an offer to study Philosophy at the Sorbonne. My essay on the Unknowable had been appreciated. I would work under an eminent professor.

Madame Marina Desmoulins and Monsieur Jean-François Desmoulins said I could come and stay with them in their home at Montmartre whenever I wanted for however long I wanted. They still missed me, even after so many months had passed. Which meant Marina missed me. Mekel Desmoulins had been registered at his adoptive father's school, the boys' *lycée* on the Rue Foyatier. Madame Marina Desmoulins was expecting another baby, Lorenzo's, of course. She was happy.

The rich Mrs Rukhsaar Anees Khan had opened a school in Azamgarh for the education and mainstreaming of girls from poor Muslim households. She wanted me to pay the school a visit. She said I had influenced her way of thinking a lot.

Madame Agnès Desmoulins had joined Monsieur Desmoulins, in Skikda. They had made a small villa for her close to their own, by the sea. It had whitewashed walls, and large bay windows overlooking the ocean. The children loved her. They called her *Petite Maman.*

Graeth was planning on returning to Paris. It was all over, he said.

The day after I left Paris, on the twenty-fifth, another building housing immigrants had been set on fire and several people had perished, including children. Then four days later, another. The count, together with the April fire, had risen to 48 dead. A small number for India but a large toll for Paris. The fires had started in the stairwells.

Then the riots happened in the fall … and Paris burned with ethnic conflict.

Things were settling down after the riots. It was in the nature of things to erupt from time to time, then to settle. The "charge" had spent itself. But human beings wouldn't change, wrote Graeth. He sent me a pertinent quote as usual, this time from Jean-Jacques Rousseau:

"To cure Humanity of itself would be to create another species"

Also read
International IMPAC Dublin Literary Award
nominated novel
My Little Boat

Three generations of free thinking women, their quests and questions:... the characters, especially the women... keep you turning the page.

— India Today